SMALL CHANGE

SMALL CHANGE

SHORTER
AND
LONGER
STORIES

by

JULIAN FANE

SINCLAIR-STEVENSON
and
ST GEORGE'S PRESS

First published in Great Britain by
Sinclair-Stevenson Limited and St George's Press
7/8 Kendrick Mews
London SW7 3HG, England

British Library Cataloguing in Publication Data
A CIP catalogue record for this book is available from the British Library.

ISBN: 1 85619 101 X

Typeset by Rowland Phototypesetting Limited
Bury St Edmunds, Suffolk
Printed and bound in Great Britain by
Butler and Tanner Limited, Frome and Somerset

Contents

Fragments

Verity I

O NCE UPON A TIME, soon after the start of the century, when I was seven years old, a sale occurred at Lyne.

On the morning of the day of the sale I was with my mother in the hall of my home, now filled with dust and piles of furniture. My mother was in sole charge – my father had gone away – and was giving the removal-men her instructions. Because I was excited and anxious to be of use, I kept on asking childish questions. She smiled wistfully and held my hand in hers, which was long and thin but also soft and warm.

Noticing a little picture behind a pillar, I pointed it out and asked: 'What about this one? Shouldn't they take this one?'

'Oh but I love that picture, darling,' she replied.

I looked at it again. It was a picture of two people, a lady and a gentleman, riding on donkeys. She rode side-saddle: one tiny booted foot peeped from beneath the skirt of her riding-habit, and she was wearing a hat with a curving feather. He wore a high top hat and smoked a cigar. The donkeys had rough coats, the landscape was grey and rocky, and the sky a most beautiful blue.

'Oh well,' my mother said to a removal-man, 'I suppose it had better go after all.'

He lifted it from the wall, exposing an ugly yellow mark.

I realised not only that I too loved the picture, but had influenced my mother to part with it. My mood abruptly changed. I felt concerned and asked: who were the people on the donkeys?

She did not know.

'It isn't so bad then, is it?'

'You don't understand,' she said.

The sale began in the afternoon. Lots and objects which failed to reach their reserves were returned from the drawing-room to the staircase hall. I sat on the stairs and listened to the gruff voice of the auctioneer, and, appreciating that if the little picture were returned my mother would be able to keep it, hoped for it to appear. I hoped and waited all afternoon, and when the sale was over searched amongst the heaps of rugs, and stacks of china, tables and chairs.

At last I went to my mother. She was sitting on the window-seat in the library, a favourite place, her head thrown back until it rested against the white and gold shutter, and turned so that she could look out at the view. Her heavily-lidded eyes were shadowed with exhaustion, her long hands folded in an un-convincing attitude of repose. As I approached she smiled with that unique sweetness which partly derived from the delicate shape of her lips. I told her the little picture had gone – her picture – my picture – and burst into tears. She tried to comfort me, without really knowing why I was upset, and although my mysterious feelings merely placed another burden on her shoulders.

Then she said: 'You mustn't allow this to happen,

4

Francis – when you're a man you mustn't ever allow this to happen again.'

The highly-strung severity of her tone, her admonition, which seemed to contain an ungrateful reference to the fault for which I was generously blaming myself, cut me to the heart. Moreover a latent fear of the day's unwonted events, in which at first I had taken so much pleasure, was brought out. I saw the sale for the disaster which in fact it was, as a threat to the security that I realised with a shock was precious to me, and a step towards the disruption of my family, home and life. And Mama apparently regarded me not as her would-be protector in these desperate circumstances, ready to share each one of her troubles and through my love to spare her the worst, but as their very instigator, and probably the engineer of their repetition.

My tears flowed more freely, my cries redoubled.

Unaware of my sense of responsibility for the fate of the little picture, unaware therefore of the unintentional effect of her overwrought warning, my mother could not calm me and eventually rang for my nurse. Upstairs, when she came to say good night, I observed through the prismatic tears her bewildered unhappy glances as she continued to misunderstand my motives. But explanation, and the unravelling of the twisted thread of our relations, were altogether beyond me. I could only embrace her with mute force, hoping that the pressure of my arms round her neck would at last let her into the secret of my feelings.

I was unsuccessful. She bade me good night. The nursery door was closed. I lay in bed and longed for the time to come when nothing would obstruct the passage of the truth from lover to beloved. For me it was always this marvellous future, so unlike the present, which was going to make up for everything, even for the incident of the picture of donkeys and bright blue sky.

The sale did not alter our style of living at Lyne. In an ochre-coloured photograph which I came across the other day, taken out-of-doors, and dated a few years before the Great War, a sizeable group is posed on the lawn encircled by the gravel sweep, in front of the balustrade that runs between the cypresses, with the pillared portico for a background. Leaning against the balustrade in rather affected attitudes of relaxation are the gentlemen guests; on the dining-room chairs sit ladies in large picture hats, beneath the weight of which their heads seem to tilt to one side, while their gloved hands rest on the long ivory handles of their parasols; behind them my great-uncle Thomas Verity, bald and bowed, but wearing a tremendous check, is being supported by Heddle, our ancient butler; on the ground at my father's feet I am sitting cross-legged, and by my mother stands my younger brother James.

Those lavish house-parties used to last for a week or ten days, and occurred all through the year. I remembered the arrival and departure of enormous so-called cabin-trunks which had hanging-space for clothes and half a dozen drawers; oddly-shaped leather top-hat-boxes; heavy flat gun-cases with metal corners; chamois-leather envelopes for soft square pillows. The ladies changed their elaborate costumes three or four times a day, and the gentlemen, who hunted and shot in the winter, and in the summer fished and played cricket,

6

tennis, golf, croquet, needed at least a dozen changes of clothes to see them through their visits. Each sex must have arrayed itself in so much finery more for its own than the opposite sex, since the ladies did not appear at breakfast and the gentlemen were engaged in their sporting pursuits for as long as it was light. They dined together, and admittedly the meal was prolonged, but afterwards the gentlemen would sit over their port and then play billiards until they went to bed.

Of course fashion always called for sacrifice, and only the representatives of a world that could afford to devote itself to fashion were pleased to receive invitations to stay with the Veritys of Lyne. The luxuries of the house were unlimited. In the outer hall there was a set of twenty-five chairs, complete with odd cups and clips at the sides, and brass-edged slots on the back-supports. The cards bearing the names of the various guests were fitted into the slots; their sticks and umbrellas were clipped into the cups; their overcoats were folded over the backs of the chairs, and their hats and caps and straw boaters laid on the flat wooden seats. In the dining-room, the distances between the candlesticks and silver objects on the table were not left to chance or the mere approval of the eye, but measured with a tape-measure before lunch and dinner. Newspapers were always being ironed to remove creases.

The highest standards were maintained both by those privileged to enjoy and by those paid to provide the luxury. I remember the indignant contempt of Heddle for a visitor with a hole in his sock. The aim of master and man was perfection, at least in outward things. For instance, at Lyne, each bedroom not only led into a husband's dressing-room, but also, by means of a door concealed in a cupboard, and in order that no errant wife

7

should have to use the public passages, into an adjoining single or 'bachelor's' room.

In the evening, by the flattering light of oil-lamps and innumerable candles, the grand ladies and gentlemen of my early childhood seem like stars to have shone most brightly. Occasionally I was allowed to watch, from the top of the stairs outside the nursery, the performance which began with Heddle sounding the gong in the hall at half-past seven.

The gong was the signal that it was time to get ready for dinner. Soon the ladies came upstairs, doubtless keen to catch a glimpse of their husbands or lovers after the separations of the day. Then I heard the gentlemen's voices, roughened by the whisky-and-soda they had drunk, and the pipes and cigars they had smoked in my father's business-room. In twos and threes they sauntered into the hall and mounted the stairs unhurriedly – they were never in a hurry – their well-cut trousers showing off the lines of their calves and fitting snugly over their neat pointed shoes.

Housemaids with white enamel cans of hot water, ladies' maids with thimbles on their fingers and dresses draped across their outstretched arms, and superior valets with suits bustled about the passages. A maid brushed marks from the red carpet on the stairs; more maids in pretty white caps with streamers and white aprons, carrying bins of fuel and cleaning materials, entered the library and drawing-room, and the octagonal room in-between, to replenish the fires, tidy the grates, polish the brass handles of doors and puff the chair cushions; footmen on step-ladders attended to the lamps and candles; and Heddle unlocked the glass-fronted letter-box and collected the scores of letters written on Lyne paper, which was thick, grey-green, and seemed to be partly made of tiny hairs.

Eventually the hall was empty and quiet, and a few of the maids, flushed from their labours, joined my nurse and me.

On such an occasion, perhaps before a ball in the neighbourhood, a certain scene was enacted, one of two scenes, to which I always return when I think of my father.

He was late. My mother and most of the house-party had already reassembled in the reception rooms. My nurse or a maid commented in a whisper on his good looks; and suddenly I was able to see that his proud and emphatic features, his distinguished figure, stood out from all I had previously admired. He crossed the threshold of the octagonal room. I was sorry to lose sight of him. But after a moment he emerged and started to pace the marble floor of the hall, as though waiting for someone. Opposite me, beyond the arches of the opposite landing, to which my attention was drawn by the glitter of a jewel, a lady – the celebrated Lady Gray, I now believe – was approaching the stairs.

Because of the formation of the staircase with its twin upper flights which unite and double back, her rustling descent was at first hidden from my father, who continued to pace impatiently and shoot his stiff cuffs, but not from me. She was wearing a dress of a glowing dark material, white gloves extending above the elbow, and diamonds. I cannot recall either her face or the colour of her hair – but her hair was surely black. Diamonds sparkled in it. There were diamonds round her neck and her wrists. The shimmering folds of silk or satin contrasted with the dead whiteness of her gloves and the living whiteness of her arms and bare shoulders, and the brilliant jewels imparted a barbaric lustre to her appearance. A quick gesture, a rearrangement of a bracelet or a ring, caused sparks and beams of reflected light to flicker in every direction.

At the halfway mark she swept to the centre of the space above the lower and wider flight of stairs, where she turned to adjust the short train of her dress. Then she looked at my father. He was standing below, his legs a little apart, head thrown up, smiling as he had never smiled at me. Her glance was prolonged, she gazed at him, and slowly, hindered perhaps by the new significance of her graceful movements, at once majestic and deferential, again began to descend.

My father raised and held out his hand. Hers, apparently almost against her will, was lifted to it. And they stayed in this picturesque position for a second or two, arrested, their fingers linked, their eyes fixed and so to speak interlocking, he with his hard expression and peculiar disturbing smile, she with her feet on different stairs, and the regal tilt of her head, and her crown of diamonds, contradicted by the submissiveness of the arm which curved meekly from her white and naked shoulder.

He said something in an undertone, at which she laughed briefly, and letting her go he followed her into the octagonal room.

Lady Gray on the staircase at Lyne, a featureless Edwardian goddess in the act of surrender, magnificent, captive, remains for me the embodiment of an era. Yet I think it was not exactly Lady Gray, although she possessed the quality of being somehow larger and more dramatic than life, which impresses children, but my

10

father, his strange feelings, that etched indelibly into my memory their meeting on the stairs.

He must have been in his mid-thirties at the time. He was tall. His hair contained a hint of red and receded slightly, his complexion seemed to glow with health and good living. The expression of his blue eyes, set wide apart under beetling reddish brows, could be clear or overcast, warm or cold. He was as kind to me as his preoccupations allowed; and if I was afraid of him I was more afraid of what he might not, than of what he might do.

He was an idealist inasmuch as he was eternally searching for that which was better than the best of everything. It was idealism of a sort that underlay his loves of women, gambling and Lyne. He loved beautiful women, but never found one whose beauty satisfied him for long; he loved money for the sake of the people and things he could spend it on, not for itself, and therefore never made any; he loved Lyne and impoverished it. He was too proud not to do his duty – 'too proud to put his stick to the ground,' as Heddle remarked – except in the case of the sale at Lyne, of which bitter consequence of his speculations he could not bear to be a witness. His servants, sensing his loyalty, his lack of arrogance, were devoted to him; he was capable of inspiring devotion as well as admiration. He probably attracted women because he could not resist them, because of his reputation, material advantages, and the natural refinement on which great charm always rests, and because of the air of detachment that rendered his spells of concentration so gratifying. They may have imagined he was harbouring some secret sorrow, which they alone could alleviate, when in fact he was worrying

11

about the result of the two-thirty at Epsom or Hurst Park.

As gambling was turned by his losses from an amusement into an only hope, and from a hope into an obsession, my father's restlessness increased. Home life was no solace to him. He needed stimulants equal to those he received from staking on race-course or Stock Exchange sums of money he could not afford. He smoked a great deal, and in the library after tea used to smoke any number of cigarettes half the way down, often bending or even breaking them between his strong fingers, as he glanced through the city and sporting pages of his crisp newspaper. Sometimes he would give me his attention, for instance telling me to blow on the lid of his gold 'hunter' watch, while he released the hidden spring, so that it opened as if by magic. Once, sitting beside him in the wagonette after a family expedition to Stonehenge, he teased me delightfully, making out that I had stolen a stone to shoot in my catapult and would have to return it by post.

The trouble was that his spirits, both high and low, were equally infectious. His ability to transmit his emotions must have constituted the chief part of his charm: it was not easy to live with. Provided he was happy everyone was happy, but at Lyne, without guests, he was more inclined to be depressed – and nobody ever advised him to cheer up or smile.

My mother excused his black moods for my benefit, saying he had a headache or was tired, as she had perhaps learnt to excuse his infidelities for her own. She was twenty-one when he married her, and not much older when he began to be unfaithful. I suppose her youth and innocence afforded her no proper hold over his experience, and her sensitive temperament, requiring tranquillity, did not permit her to indulge the passion for excitement to which he was already committed. She continued to honour and obey, and love too in her undemanding fashion, the stranger and husband from whom nothing but death would part her, and found her true vocation in the care of their children.

That was why, on hearing of the birth of James, who was five years younger than me, I cried, sorry to have to share with another her intense affection. But I grew fond of my little brother, and not merely in imitation of Mama – or at any rate liked to entertain him with tales of a terrifying giant, whose name I have forgotten. The giant was modelled to some extent on my great-uncle Thomas, my father's uncle and my last surviving relative of that generation, the gentleman wearing the tremendous check in the photograph, who, despite his age and infirmities, would hunt me round the nursery table, tapping his ebony stick against the legs of chairs.

James was never able to say no to the frightful thrill of listening to my tales. He even urged me to tell him more. They became a first bond between us, a realisation of our visions of life. In them two boys, two brothers, guessed that their home was in danger, and erected barricades, dug pits, set ingenious traps, and looked on their finished work with satisfaction, believing themselves secure. But the giant advanced, breaking down the park wall and scattering defences far and wide; the grown-ups, who had not heeded the warnings of the boys, were taken unawares; all fled, in fear and dissension; and the brothers were estranged.

The giant represented everything of which we were afraid, the evil powers surrounding us, the outside world beyond the park wall of Lyne, the irresistible dictates of fate. He was the destroyer of our happiness and our achievements. The terror, the horror especially resided in the contrast between the brothers' belief that they were safe and the discovery of their error, the blame, anger, quarrels and estrangement.

My departure for school, now rapidly approaching, may have been responsible for the accent on safety or security in these disastrous narratives. I dared not confess my actual fears except in the context of the story of the giant, and usually at night, in the dark, to a scared and uncomprehending James. I dared not confess them to my mother, but expected her to show by some loving sign that they were appreciated. I was ready to suffer, more than ready, so long as my suffering was known and my courage recognised. It was therefore disappointing to observe, gazing into her shadowed eyes, standing in front of her as she rested on the window-seat in the library, that to her customary tenderness of expression was joined not acknowledgment of my brave response to my situation, but a worried question, a plea for the answer that all was well with me, which I refused to give.

My silence, my disappointment ensured hers. She also must have longed for her reserve to be robustly brushed aside. If I had been able to tell her the truth, although she seemed not to want it, had said that I was sorry but I was unhappy and afraid to go to school, she would have been entirely sympathetic. But I could not tell her anything, could not put into words my difficult and mortifying feelings, without the encouragement which she, wishing neither to offend against our unwritten family laws of privacy, nor to increase my suspected unhappiness by any reference to it, was careful not to offer.

She tried to distract me. We made expeditions – it must have been at this time we went to Stonehenge. She probably hoped I would learn to follow her example and find pleasure in the midst of pain, but my masculine nature, my childish absolutism, denied me every consolation. Laughter itself was enough to make me sad, by reminding me that shortly I would have nothing to laugh at. Yet when she enquired if I was enjoying myself and received an equivocal reply, and her smiling lips contracted, her hand was removed from my shoulder, and she turned reproachfully away, I would recall the story of the giant and accept with a mere sense of having been proved right a state of affairs from which in my imagination I had already extracted most of the grief.

And some hours spent with Mama and James beside the lakes, under the leaning trees and within the sound of the waterfall, still contained the element of peaceful unclouded joy characteristic of my childhood at Lyne.

But James, a few weeks before the date of my departure, fell ill. His illness, which was serious – my mother was always in his room – altered him. He had gone to bed my junior in every respect; he returned to the nursery almost as tall as I was, with his face lengthened and a look in his eyes that disconcerted me. One evening we were in the library. My father was not present, and my mother sat at the piano, picking out the accompaniment to the song 'Drink to me only', which she wanted James to sing. I remember he was wearing a sailor-suit, fitted out with lanyard and whistle, that the darkness of the uniform accentuated the pale fragility of his features and slender neck, and that he stood on one side of Mama's high-backed chair, while I stood on the other.

James had a small sweet voice, unlike me, and at a nod

began to sing: 'Drink to me only with thine eyes, And I will pledge with mine . . .'

I kept on interrupting. Mama lost her patience and told me to be quiet. To add to the misery which had made me interrupt, I now for the first time felt a pang of jealousy, mixed with self-pity, because I had not been ill, and had to go to school, and could not sing, and was told to be quiet.

And in my misery and self-pity and jealousy of James, I reached round the chair and gave him a push which knocked him over, He started to cry. I grew generally angry, not least with myself, so that when Mama, after picking up James, scolded me, I simply turned my back on her.

She declared that I was rude, unkind, and obviously did not care, referring perhaps not only to my recent conduct but also to my obstinate refusal to talk about school.

I agreed hotly, as though wishing her to complete my catastrophe: she was absolutely right, I did not care.

'Oh Francis!' she exclaimed.

'But Fra's unhappy,' James wailed. 'Fra's unhappy, Mama — don't you see?'

The scene ends with my recollection of his sudden wail. His perception of my motives, his forgiveness of my spiteful action, blotted from my memory immediately subsequent events. I was amazed and moved to gratitude by his intervention on my behalf, which marked both the starting-point of our closer union and the real break between my childhood and boyhood; but afterwards I could not easily feel free with my brother. His eyes seemed to uncover my secret thoughts, naturally and mysteriously, without prying, and to establish a criterion, a moral standard, below which I was apt to fall. And for all his intentions never to judge me, I was forced to read in his true regard, old beyond his years, the faithful record of my successes and many failures.

Some days later I descended the stairs, with none of the assurance of Lady Gray, although my father awaited me at the bottom, to say goodbye to my family. I too walked slowly for my different reasons, by the balustrade, holding in one hand my strapped tartan rug, and in the other an attaché-case, my parting gift from Mama. My father watched me, bending slightly forward from the waist, until I stood before him on the marble floor, studying his highly polished shoes.

'Listen, Francis,' he said.

I raised my head, as though about to answer: 'No, Father, no – you must listen!'

But he caught me with his blue unflinching glance, and I said nothing.

After a second's pause, during which I searched his face, hoping to find in it some miraculous message of reprieve, he continued: 'Listen, when things have to be done we try to do them well, and without complaining, don't we?'

Such was the power of his personality that even in this crisis and in spite of myself I nodded my agreement. Under the portico I said goodbye to Heddle, and without disgracing anyone kissed my nurse, James, Mama, and finally my father. Then I climbed onto the green leather seat of the wagonette and was driven away from Lyne.

*

17

In the summer of the third year of the war, when I was fifteen and James ten, our father came home on leave.

His other leaves must have occurred during my school terms. Now with Mama and James I was able to meet him at the station. He stepped out of the train. I was relieved to see that his spare uniformed figure was as upright, his bearing as distinguished as ever. Driving to Lyne, while we talked to him excitedly, he listened, asked questions and laughed at our eagerness to answer. But after half-an-hour in the library he appeared to grow restless, tossed the cigarette which he had just lit into the fireplace, and interrupted our conversation to turn and watch it smouldering in the grate. And his abrupt gesture, combined with the suddenly strained expression on Mama's face, brought back to me in a rush all the forgotten difficulties of living with my father.

Those difficulties had increased. He was more than restless, although to myself I still described his moods of urgent disquiet in the former simpler way. The years in France had marked him. And perhaps he had a premonition of the financial reckoning with which the end of the war, if he should live to celebrate it, threatened – not to mention the already encroaching effects of the ageing process. Yet in the library, having tossed his cigarette into the fire and watched it absorbedly for a few moments, he looked up smiling, his eyes apologetic, as though sorry for the silence he had imposed on us. James and I were urged by Mama to leave the room: our father was tired by his journey and wished to be left alone.

But he said: 'No, no, Emm,' shortening her Christian name Emma, as was his habit. 'Don't send them away. I'd like to have a bath and a change. Let the boys stay down to dinner.'

All the evenings he was at Lyne, including the last, before the party, James and I dined with our parents. For Mama, although she had been separated from her husband for months, his request that we should dine downstairs was not so much a slight to her vanity as a charming compliment. She used to come along to our rooms before dinner to make sure we were ready, our hair brushed, our nails clean. On that first evening I wore a new blue suit she had given me. My father observed – but tactfully – that the collar might be cut a little too high. She was stricken. Each of his corrections of our dress and manners represented a fault found with her, the steward of our upbringing, on which she had expended infinite care and effort, just as every sign of his condescension towards us represented her reward.

About half-past nine, when our meal was finished, she would take James up to bed. My father, dressed in a smoking-suit of brown or royal blue velvet, with slippers to match, rose and accompanied them to the door, kissed James on the top of his head, smiled and nodded at Mama, and returned to the chair that Heddle stood behind. There were two or three such quiet evenings, on which he did not ask any guests to dinner. Although he may have meant to discuss the affairs of the estate with his son and heir, in fact he spent most of the time talking to his butler. The red-shaded candles in their branching candlesticks shone on the gleaming surface of the table, the silver models of pheasants and partridges, the maple-wood cigar-box, and the ribbed glass bowls containing those slow-burning matches never seen nowadays. I poured out my half-glass of port, professionally shaking the last drop from the lip of the decanter. And my father, who loved women but preferred the company of men, inquired as he clipped the end of his cigar and tried it between his teeth: 'Well – how are things, Heddle?'

He expected people to accept their positions in the world, as he accepted the advantages and disadvantages of his own. He despised the vulgar pretensions and resentments of the members of any class. He and Heddle could talk together freely. They were tried and trusted friends. But if anyone should offend against his code of good behaviour, he or she would be punished with the haughtiest scorn. One evening an applicant for the post of agent at Lyne, who had been invited to dinner, remarked after the ladies had left the dining-room: 'These are grand cigars, Sir Gerald – where do you get them?' My father's response, a silent icy stare, frightened me nearly as much as it frightened his questioner. I remember marvelling at the foolhardy courage of Germans, who actually dared to fight against him.

Instead of seeking in the modern manner for the psychological explanation of conduct, a search which tends to diminish the individual's responsibility for his actions, my father, contemptuous of excuses and complaints, always judged by appearances.

With Heddle on those evenings I recall, he loved to talk of days gone by, of St John's, the Verity house in London, in Regent's Park, which he had been forced to sell. At St John's the family had once spent the months of the social season. 'There was pasture for cattle and sheep,' the old man would remind him; 'we used to take the cattle and sheep from Lyne every summer.' Sometimes my father roughly changed the subject, as though he could not bear to talk of that period, when he was young and had not yet squandered his inheritance. He would tap the ash from his cigar and restlessly push his chair away from the table.

'Look at the boy – he's fast asleep,' Heddle would say.

It was true that the port, the warmth, the voices, and a sense of security which only my father's presence in the house conferred upon me, had begun to play tricks on my sight and hearing, so that my empty glass seemed to change its shape and interminable minutes to elapse between each utterance. But I exclaimed loudly that I was not in the least tired. My father smiled and said: 'Come on, you ought to be in bed. Good night, Heddle.' Then, standing up, he would drain his single glass of brandy, call the dogs, whistling through his teeth, throw his cigar into the low fire, and leave the room with the customary quick decisiveness of all his movements.

He must have been at home for the best part of a week when there occurred the second of the two scenes that especially remain in my memory, the companion-piece to the scene on the stairs at Lyne.

It was a wonderful August morning. We were walking along the path on the far side of the bottom lake. The contrast between the bright reflection of sun on the water, and the thick shade cast by the overhanging boughs of trees, dazzled my eyes, and I had to exert myself to keep up with my father, who strode ahead of me, wearing a check suit with narrow trousers rolled above the ankle and a coat cut very long and loose.

I was honoured to be asked to accompany him on his daily tours of the estate. But during those tours I could never think of anything to say, while he scarcely spoke to me. And on this particular morning he walked so gloomily, now and again slashing with his thumb-stick at stray nettles, seemed in such a hurry, as though he wished to outdistance me, and in my inexact terminology was so restless, that I began to suffer more acutely than before from the feelings of disappointment, and of inadequacy, which he had inspired intermittently ever since his return.

Anyhow, by the fishing-house, a little folly built on the edge of the lake, as we were coming to it, we heard the sound of a horse's hooves along the drive, falling irregularly on the stony surface, slow and then fast. My father stopped and looked at me, listening; and his face, either because the hot sunlight in which we were now standing shone on it, or because of the prospect of a distraction – catching a stray horse, warning off a trespasser – seemed to relax. He turned and led the way into the fishing-house, but before opening the other door, which gave onto the drive, told me to hold his dog, a labrador called Bill, in case he should run out. I slipped my handkerchief through Bill's collar – the door was opened – we emerged once more into the sunlight and saw at a distance of twenty-five yards, seated side-saddle on a horse that shook its long mane and advanced towards us diagonally, a young woman wearing a brown riding-habit.

My father asked who she was. Mrs Vernon, I answered. I had met her. She was a war-widow, and had recently taken Old Acre, one of the houses in the village. He nodded, knowing the name, and, directing me to stay with Bill on the grass verge, moved into the centre of the drive, where he stood with his hand resting on his thumb-stick and his body tensed forwards from the waist. The horse, glimpsing him out of the corner of a rolling eye, half-reared, half-twisted to one side, so that the light filtering through the leaves of the trees dappled its shiny flank. Then, as the rider swayed, attempting to regain her balance, it faced my father squarely and trotted at him, throwing out its front hooves in an alarming fashion. I thought he must be trodden underfoot – Mrs Vernon was leaning back, straining unsuccessfully at the reins. But with his raised free hand he neatly caught the bridle, clung to it for a few dragging steps, and brought the animal to a halt.

Nobody spoke for a moment. The horse shook its head violently, snorting and breathing hard. Mrs Vernon gathered her reins and glanced at my father, an expression on her face I could not interpret. The comparative arrest of movement, the oddly prolonged silence of the group five yards away, for some reason increased my preceding excitement.

At length, in a tone of voice I had never heard him use, soft and mocking, my father said: 'Your horse is fresh.'

The lady compressed her rather full lips. I was afraid she was going to strike at him with her elegant light-coloured switch. But nothing so melodramatic took place.

She merely remarked: 'I could have managed quite well without your help. Thank you just the same.'

Ignoring her apparent displeasure, which did not seem to put him out at all, my father continued in his mocking voice: 'Would you like my boy to fetch your hat?'

She could not have known it was missing, for she lifted her gloved hand as though to feel for it, and looked up as though to catch sight of its brim. Her gestures, appealing in their spontaneity, made me realise that the apparently nondescript tenant of Old Acre, to whom one day in the estate office I had been introduced, was in fact a handsome woman with splendid pale blue eyes.

Finding the hat was not where it should have been, she said almost sullenly: 'Oh!' – then asked, showing her large teeth in a pretty smile, as she at once admitted her defeat and coquettishly tried to turn it into a victory: 'Am I speaking to my landlord?'

No doubt she had entered the park in the hope of such an encounter, had lost control of her horse, and had been flustered and annoyed to have done so, unbecomingly, in front of the man she wanted to meet. But grasping the advantage her difficulties after all afforded her, she apologised with an attractive show of confusion for trespassing, blamed her horse, which she called Tiger – 'You see, Tiger always decides where we're going' – and gratefully accepted my father's offer to escort her home. I was told to fetch the missing hat, for which service I received the favour of a wide and brilliant smile, and another introduction to its owner, and was left with Bill to watch Tiger being led along the drive bleached by sunlight. My father turned to talk to Mrs Vernon, who leant forwards and sideways to hear what he was saying, and straightened her back in its shapely brown habit and laughed gaily. Her laughter, along with the jingle of the bridle and the cries of woodland birds, drifted on the waves of heat, until muffled by the heavy summer atmosphere in the same way that the horse and rider and retreating figure, framed by the arching trees and camouflaged by flecks of green and gold light, were absorbed little by little into the natural haze of the background.

Regretfully, for I wished the scene could have gone on for ever, I returned to the house. It struck me that the labrador Bill and I were linked not only by my handkerchief through his collar, but also by an admiration for my father in which there were no more reservations. The episode in the drive revealed anew his courage and resourcefulness, his charm, capable of transforming the deepest displeasure into gay laughter, and the reserved and therefore incalculable power of his personality, which could never again disappoint me.

But when he came home to lunch in high spirits, Mama, to whom I had described the events of the morning in enthusiastic detail, remarked sharply across the dining-room table: 'I'm told you saved the life of that woman from Old Acre.'

'Francis has been exaggerating,' he replied.

I began to protest on his behalf as well as my own. But he advised me not to talk too much. As the meal proceeded I was at least pleased to see that my mother, after appearing to overcome some inward obstacle, exposed herself to the contagion of his unusually sunny humour. She may have been thankful for the small mercy of an improvement of his state of mind, whoever or whatever was the cause of it. And perhaps, for her as indeed for everyone else, that first and last sign of a jealousy she knew was useless ushered in a happier time, since it denoted her abandonment of the vain hope, raised by separation, that she and her husband could obtain from their affections for each other any true gratification of their incompatible desires.

Of course at Lyne, in the ensuing days, we saw less of him than before. He was out a lot. He went racing. He found he had to be in London for a couple of nights. But we enjoyed the odd hours he spared us, filled as they were with his dry jokes and suddenly boyish laughter, and were really too busy to miss him, preparing for the party to be held on the last evening of his leave.

He had suggested the party, probably because he wished to spend that evening, the right of his family, in the company of Mrs Vernon, whose presence amongst our other neighbours could not be remarked upon. He had even been induced to lend me an old dinner jacket, not too bad a fit, selected from the coveted lines of suits in his extensive cupboards. The drawing-room, where we were going to dance, was cleared of furniture. The brown holland coverings were removed from the chandeliers, the oak floor was polished and sprinkled with French chalk. Invitations were sent out, flowers were brought in. And on the afternoon of the day of the party, to which I was looking forward with mixed feelings of dread and feverish excitement, the cloudless blue of the sky promised a fine summer's night.

James and I were dressed by seven o'clock. We slid about together on the dancing-floor, dodging the mossy tiers of pot-plants, the scents of which were wafted through the house. But as the time of arrival of the dinner-guests drew near, I surrendered to anxiety, left James to his irresponsible devices, and waited in the hall. Eventually my father came downstairs in his faultless black and white clothes. I remember, when he smiled at me – his face freshly shaved and rosy from his bath – my gratitude for the sense of well-being he spread around, and my wonder that he, the host, should be so confident. Our guests were announced. We went in to dinner. And the pleasure I began to extract from watching him at the end of the table, sitting between ladies who grew animated as soon as he turned their way, was only undermined by the speaking glances of my mother, imploring me to behave well and say something to those condemned to sit next to me.

A little later, after I had drunk my ration of port, listening with one flattered ear to the conversation of the gentlemen, and with the other, apprehensively, to the band tuning up behind the drawing-room door, I saw my mother greet Mrs Vernon. The latter, talking to a tall soldier, followed the line of guests into the staircase hall and, as she queued to shake hands, darted a swift appraising glance at her hostess. Mama was wearing a dress of a metallic blue colour; Mrs Vernon's was white, diaphanous, décolletée, with a pattern of big red flowers. The two women confronted each other, smiling their difficult and easy smiles, and I was depressed to notice the chilliness of Mama's manner, and the mere refinement of her appearance, in comparison with the vivid looks of my father's friend.

Mrs Vernon shook hands with him, smiling more widely – she seemed about to burst into laughter – and pursued by the soldier swept through the open doors of the octagonal room. The candle-light suffused the powdered flesh of her shoulders with a golden glow, and the band, as though to express its admiration of her beauty, started to play.

Meanwhile I was isolated in the midst of the crowded fascinating scene, and apparently for the rest of the evening. Yet when Mama brought over and introduced a girl called Rose Fernwood, I felt furious with her first for obviously taking pity on my lonely state, then for pitilessly leaving me alone in the company of a total stranger. I had no alternative except to ask the girl to dance in order to break some interminable silence, and we entered the drawing-room.

It turned out she was not a total stranger. I had danced with her several times for want of others to dance with, because it was easier to dance in silence than sit in it, and less humiliating than having to talk to James or pretend that Heddle had engaged me in earnest conversation. All of a sudden Rose Fernwood informed me we had met before, years and years before at a children's party. There was a snapshot of me in her mother's book, she said, wearing woollen leggings and a moleskin cap, and standing by a goldfish pond with a stick in my hand. The unexpected view of my younger self inspired in me a feeling of tenderness. I even felt tender towards this foolish girl, who had kept by her for so many years the undeniably charming memory of a boy in a moleskin cap; and I became aware of her trim shoes with buckles, her white stockings and white dress threaded with pink ribbon, her extraordinarily long and thin arms, and the fair hair worn down her back which tickled my hand during our dances.

In one of the intervals we sat on the stairs and ate ices, I very slowly, she in a flash. I asked if it did not give her a headache, to eat an ice so quickly. Yes, she replied, it always did, but she liked that sort of headache. She spoke in such a definite way, then seemed so abashed by the strength of her opinion, that I laughed, causing her to blush, lower her blue reproachful eyes, finally to laugh too, but uncertainly, as though she could not quite believe that she was able to amuse me. We parted; but after I had taken James up to bed, had been reassured by his passionate protests that I was lucky to return to the party, and drunk a glass of champagne and danced with Mama, we got together again and strolled out-of-doors.

And we met my father. We had strolled to the bridge between the lakes and turned back to the house. Music mingled with the sounds of the waterfall, and on the sloping lawns silhouettes of dancing couples revolved in the distorted rectangles of illumination thrown through the open drawing-room windows. He was alone, striding down the path in our direction. He stopped and asked Rose if she was having a good time. She answered inaudibly, allowing her long arms to droop, and awkwardly clasping her hands in front of her dress. I began to say it was a lovely party, but he interrupted, inquiring for Mrs Vernon: had I seen her, was she by the bridge? His face, with the lights of the house behind it, had been in shadow; but now he moved, so that I was able partly to observe, partly to deduce from his questions, its hard impatient lines. And as in the library on the day of his arrival, and particularly on the morning of the episode in the drive, I was once more struck by his terrible restlessness.

I said no, no, I had not seen Mrs Vernon – bewildered by the change that had occurred in him since he came down the stairs before dinner. She was not by the bridge, he repeated. No, I said, feeling inadequate. He thanked me, summoned a slight smile, and retreated towards the terrace.

I was too constrained, too dissatisfied with myself, with Mrs Vernon who had disappeared, with Rose Fernwood who was no more than an embarrassment and an encumbrance, with the whole evening, to re-enter the house immediately. I therefore led Rose into the garden, to a seat in the tent-like arbour under the weeping-willow tree. We had been sitting for a few minutes below the parapet of the terrace, but hidden from it, when we heard my father's voice. Very distinct in spite of being pitched low, it contained, as well as the possessive inflexions to which I paid scarcely any attention, a note of infectious relief.

'Where have you been?'

A woman's voice murmured a reply.

'But you must tell me where!'

Mrs Vernon claimed fluently: 'Looking for you.'

'Where?'

'By the bridge.'

It was not true. She had never been by the bridge. I would have seen her there.

After a slight pause, in a tone of angry resignation, as though at this late stage of his leave he could not afford to expose her lie or quarrel, he said: 'You can do better than that.'

Sulkily, but with more care, she declared: 'I don't know where I've been – I've been looking for you everywhere.'

Silence fell. I thought they must have moved away. But peering through the branches of the willow tree I saw in the semi-darkness above the line of the terrace parapet – not two yards from me – the white of a shirt-front and the softer white of a diaphanous dress.

'Come!' he exclaimed, making me jump, and I heard footsteps and the receding swish of a skirt across the paving.

I stood up, blushing hotly, less because of the intimacy of the exchange on which Rose and I had eavesdropped, than because my father and his friend were together, and at last I felt free to yield to the previously inhibited excitement that had expressed itself in dread, unfair fury with Mama, dissatisfaction, and indecision as to whether or not I was enjoying the party. I stood up, without having grasped the meaning of the scene on the terrace, and asked Rose to dance. She accepted, blushing too – she had probably understood more than me of what we had overheard – and followed me into the house.

I suppose refreshments were being served, for although the band played the drawing-room was empty except for Mrs Vernon and my father, who danced close, in half-time to the music, in the centre of the floor. Rose and I circled round them, catching glimpses now of his set face, now of hers with its acquiescent smile, seeing now his dark straight back, now hers, automatically flexing to meet his demands. Her act of undefined betrayal, his inability to monopolise her affections, and the end of their affair, his party, his leave – all described the fate overtaking my father, of which I was oblivious. Faster and faster I danced round the room, flying lightly and sure-footedly from one flashing landmark to another – the flowers – the band – the double-doors – the two central figures – bearing Rose Fernwood on the wings of my excitement and happiness. For he held in his arms the object of his search, while I held in mine a companion not just absurdly shy and overgrown, but amusing, sweet, in fact entrancing, who gripped my hand with a pleasant sticky pressure and laughed out loud as we successfully turned the corners.

But the music finished and my father, passing me, responded to my smile by saying in his coldest tone of voice: 'Why aren't you in bed?'

Soon afterwards, hurt and mystified, and having got rid of Rose, I found Mama and kissed her good night.

Early the next morning my father joined me in the dining-room, evidently tired. I had seen his patent-leather shoes on the table outside the butler's pantry. They were covered with the yellow dust peculiar to the drive at Lyne. And in the course of future reflections it came to me that after some sort of reconciliation with Mrs Vernon he must have walked home from Old Acre in the dawn.

At breakfast that morning, having drunk a cup of coffee, he lowered his paper and remarked, clearing his throat: 'Francis, I'm afraid the family finances are in a bit of a muddle.'

I was taken by surprise, as I had been by his unkind exclamation on the dancing-floor, and again recognised the unsuitable pain and confusion in his eyes. Yet instead of shock, instead of sympathy, I felt a revolutionary upsurge of resentment. Our movement away from each other, begun the previous evening, when I had kept on misunderstanding him, and had imagined my climax of happiness was based upon his, could not be arrested. And for his part in this process of detachment, for the pity he now seemed to force upon me, I was suddenly unable to forgive him.

He threw the paper onto the floor, stood up, crossed over to the window, produced the 'hunter' watch from his waistcoat pocket – he was changing into uniform in London – and said he would soon have to go.

But he continued: 'No – I'm afraid I haven't looked after things too well.'

I replied to the effect that I was sure he had, wishing he would go at once.

He said: 'I wanted you to know I'm sorry. You'd better learn a lesson from my life.'

He pressed the spring of the watch so that the lid flew open, studied its dial, frowning, and turned abruptly, left the room and mounted the stairs to bid my mother goodbye.

For ten minutes or so, in the staircase hall where the trestle-tables of the night before and some gilded chairs were stacked, I waited for him with James and with Heddle, who carried his summer overcoat of a grey, almost lavender-colour material, his grey gloves, his hat and his stick. Because I was unwilling to explore my new feelings I felt nothing, except perhaps the forlorn hope that I was wrong, that with a careless word or gesture my father would replace our relations on their old unequal footing, and I would simply be able to look up to him with my former unbounded admiration. But he descended the stairs so slowly, and his face was so pale and drawn, that he reminded me of myself on the morning of my first departure for school.

Heddle helped him with his coat. We followed him into the outer hall. The sun was shining through the windows onto the worn marble of the floor. He shook hands with Heddle, and under the portico, beside the wagonette which he still liked to use, although there were cars in the coach-house, embraced James and me. Then in a manner I could unreservedly admire – arm thrown stylishly forward, head tilted – he put on his hat.

For a moment I believed I was safe – he would leave me with my unsullied memory of the way he wore his hat.

But he gazed at the enclosed view of the park he loved, the top lake and meadows set among rising wooded hills, and said in a strange clear voice, louder than necessary: 'Francis, look after everything for me.'

His request, more of a plea than a command, caused to well up within me both the intolerable pity I had experienced over breakfast and my consequent and unforgiving resentment. I kicked at a stone in silence, my hands in my pockets. He climbed into the wagonette, said a word to the groom and started to drive away.

I wished to tell him that I would look after everything, would always do my best, but the wagonette was already sweeping round on the far side of the balustrade. My mother must have come to an upstairs window to wave goodbye, for before the rhododendrons hid him from view he turned towards the house for the last time, and raised his eyes and smiled, his grey coat gathered loosely about him, the brim of his hat cutting across his forehead at an angle.

A week later we heard he had been killed.

A memorial service was held in the chapel, attended by most of the people who had been at his party. After it, a friend I did not recognise at once, dressed all in black, wearing a thick veil, through which I eventually distinguished the features of Mrs Vernon, approached me. She laid her hand on my shoulder with that gentle roughness of women who are used to men, and said in a choking voice, while the tears streamed down her cheeks: 'You're like your father – you should be proud!'

She hurried on; others spoke to me. But her sentiment penetrated the defences against emotion on which the impact of my father's death had as yet made hardly any impression – and I do not include the dishonourable thought that I was the heir to his title and home, and cupboards full of clothes. A gap opened in those defences, a breach, which time was only to widen. I began to mourn my father, loved as youth loves, selfishly, for what I wanted him to be rather than for what he was, and without knowing my love until it was too late.

Verity II

M Y MOTHER BORE the shock of widowhood with touching fortitude. Her marriage had not been truly successful or happy; but there were reasons beyond its success and happiness to make her suffer when death brought it to a conclusion. She had lost if not a passionate lover, or even a close companion, at least the arbiter of her days, whether he was absent or present, and the involuntary trembling of her lips gave new meaning to the high-flown hackneyed phrases in current use, which she uttered in reply to the sympathetic overtures of many friends.

Her dignity and patient courage, and efforts to spare others the spectacle of her grief, won from me the solicitude and protectiveness which I had been apt to refuse on previous occasions, when she appealed for protection. Together we made the necessary arrangements and went up to London to see the family lawyer. My father had not exaggerated about the state of his finances, as events were too soon to prove. Yet in his will he left a generous annuity to my mother, numerous bequests to his employees, and instructions to me to provide fairly for my younger brother.

We tried to respect his wishes with regard to the servants; but in most cases their legacies were also their farewell presents. Luckily Heddle did not live to see the inevitable changes at Lyne, to which he could not have grown accustomed. His end seemed to accentuate the facts that my father and his world were indeed no more, that ease and security belonged to the past, and that I would soon have to go to the war, facts on the reverse side of the medal of my inheritance, such as it was, from contemplation of which I continued to extract a materialistic thrill. At Heddle's funeral my sense of bereavement and vulnerability filled my eyes with unexpected tears, though whether on account of our butler, my father, or myself, I did not know.

Another change, another link cut, was the departure of Mrs Vernon from Old Acre. News of Sir Gerald Verity's gallant reputation may have attracted her to the village of Lyne, as it was probably responsible for her ride in the park, wearing her fetching brown habit. My father's reputation was such that in later life I was frequently the recipient of feminine attention, glances suddenly interested, and either softened by a sweet reminiscence or emboldened by a distant desire, which he and not I had merited. But although Mrs Vernon may have come to Lyne in a merely adventurous spirit of conquest, to be loved by my father and deceive him whenever it pleased her to do so, I believe she left a scene in which she had been conquered, at any rate to the extent of weeping violently at his memorial service, perhaps with remorse for having lied to him about the bridge.

Her laughter, which had drifted and echoed in the drive, became a memory for me. Her dress with its red flowers, her untruthful voice on the terrace, her supple dancing to the music of the period, her hand laid on my shoulder outside the chapel, became memories. The shutters were closed at Old Acre, preparatory to our disposal of the property; and shutters closed with a certain finality in many of the rooms at Lyne. For once, I left home to return to my public school with a feeling of relief. In a measured exchange of letters with Mama, in routine and work, I could at least temporarily forget the war and the responsibilities bearing down upon me.

Meanwhile James, thanks to his age, or rather to his youth, was spared my worst worries. He was still at his first educational establishment. Perhaps he was also lucky in that he was out of range of my contradictory feelings for the three annual school terms.

If the origin of the trouble between us was his insight into my motives, when because of his sailor-suit and his singing I had pushed him onto the floor, and he had explained to Mama that I was unhappy, a later scene on a winter's day, one Christmas holidays, describes the developing state of our relations.

On the occasion in question we were collecting wood for a bonfire beyond the garden wall. I must have been on the terrace, for I remember being both above and at some distance from James, who was trudging across from the top lake at Lyne, over the icy water-meadows and patches of snow and exposed black earth. It was growing dark, but the hot stream of his breath was visible as he laboured under the weight of a huge log, his thin legs in tight breeches and stockings straining, his muddy boots which looked too big for him slipping in all directions. I ran down the steps and through the garden to help him, seeing in his small figure not merely an unnecessary appendage, too young and ignorant ever to be numbered amongst the select company of my friends at school, but my one and only brother, and a vital part of the dear familiar landscape, stilled by the frost of twilight.

He seemed to understand my altered feelings – he understood everything – and responded with a mixture of bashfulness and wide-eyed pleasure. We lit the bonfire, and after tea watched through the library windows the flames leaping over the terrace wall and the bright orange sparks soaring upwards. But then some extra eagerness on his part aroused in me the desire to tease, torment him, and play upon his incautious confidence in my friendship.

That episode was succeeded by others of the same sort. On the roof at Lyne I taught him how to smoke. Behind a chimney on a sunny day I would light our stolen cigarettes, show him how to inhale, and blow jets of smoke out of my nose and mouth simultaneously. When James tried to follow my example, exclaiming that he wished he could do it like me, I would ask if he felt all right – he looked pretty green, was he going to be sick? He used to smoke in my bedroom at night, sitting on the window-seat in his dressing-gown, with the moonlight intermittently illuminating one side of his face. I cannot remember all I told him on those confidential nights, the dreams and feelings never so freely expressed, which would be safe in his loyal keeping. Yet even our moonlight communion was bedevilled by an intrusive spirit of cruelty.

For instance, after my father's death, I was inclined to say that I too might be killed in the war. Fear of the army, of life in the trenches and wounds, possibly mortal, had become my increasing preoccupation. James would tell me not to be silly, and insist that I was not going to get killed, at once with a conviction which relieved my anxiety and a provocative concern.

'But I might very well, James – Father was. It's no good being sentimental. It's no good pretending. I'm sure you've thought of all this. I'd just like to know what you intend to do with Lyne when it's yours.'

He would contradict me, promise he had not thought of anything, swear that he had no plans for Lyne, until at last he relapsed into sorrowful silence and turned his head away; and I would hasten to say in a voice from which the remorselessly reasonable quality was removed that I had been joking about our inheritance, would not let myself be killed, and was truly sorry.

But my brother's gift of being able to transmute defeat into victory cost him dear, for each of his defeats had to be experienced before his victories could be obtained, and if I was always vanquished by his beautifully clear feelings he was greatly oppressed by my confused ones. Without knowing why, against my inclinations and even my will, I attacked what I wished to defend and worsened relations I was hoping to improve, and my bad behaviour gave James the chance to behave unforgivably well, and so on in a vicious circle. The apparently deliberate choice of his disposition, rather to suffer at my hands than not to spoil me, constituted a constant temptation and a challenge I was powerless to resist.

All the same I could go too far. Once, yielding to the repeated requests of Mama, I agreed to take him out shooting. The idea of shooting with James had always bored me, no doubt because he was so keen to be initiated into the mysterious pleasures of my chief interest and pastime. We walked up to Beechwood together. While collecting the guns from the gun-room he had

39

trembled with excitement and giggled, and now he talked a lot and kept on asking stupid questions, to which, it seemed to me, in view of the fact that he had received shooting lessons from the gamekeeper, he ought to have known the answers.

When we reached the edge of the wood I positioned him behind a tree, told him to wait for the pigeons that would soon fly in to roost, and went to another tree about a hundred yards away. After a few moments I heard a single shot and the fall of a bird through the branches. His success astonished me. In a determined attempt at least to equal it, I tried too hard to shoot the four or five pigeons that came within range and consequently missed them. Then, realising I had heard no more shots from James since the first, although the pigeons had continued to fly over his tree, I left my hiding-place and hurried along to see what had happened to him. He was sitting on his cartridge-bag in an attitude of dejection, his gun on the ground beside him, a dead pigeon lying at his feet.

My anxiety that he might have hurt himself immediately gave way to the mounting irritation it had merely interrupted, which was not allayed by his inquiry: 'Did you get any, Fra?'

I answered no, and demanded an explanation of what he thought he was doing.

'I didn't want to go on,' he said, and added, his eyes expressing both his wish to trust me and his fear that I was not to be trusted; 'I had to kill the pigeon, it was wounded.'

For some reason, because it was my practice to behave towards him unpredictably, or because his tenderheartedness and integrity commanded my temporary respect, I confined myself to saying fairly sympathetically, but in such a way as to place on his shoulders the responsibility for ruining my afternoon, that in that case we had better return home.

Mama met us at Lyne, saw the pigeon, which I was carrying, and began to congratulate me on having shot it. I told her she must congratulate James. She did so with – to my mind – excessive warmth, probably intending to encourage his sporting instincts. My brother glanced at me apologetically, confessed that his single shot had been a fluke, that he had not even meant to kill the pigeon, that he had hated having to finish it off, and said that in future he would prefer not to shoot but just to keep me company on my shooting expeditions, the idea of which seemed to attract him as much as ever. By this time the part of myself that had feared for his safety, that appreci-ated and respected him, had been ousted by the other part which had to take advantage of his foolhardy truth-fulness; which chose to see in his humble appeal about the future all sorts of arrogant claims on my patience; which bitterly blamed him for spoiling everything; and, in short, was furious with him, furiously jealous.

I laughed harshly and exclaimed in reply, addressing Mama, that he had really carried on too ridiculously, was too soft and squeamish, really an absolute baby! And he had been nothing but a nuisance the whole afternoon, and was not going to keep me company out shooting – he could go with somebody else!

He sulked. I do not remember for how long on this particular occasion he sulked. Sometimes for days on end he would maintain his distant and deadly politeness, and nothing would alter his mournful demeanour, broaden his rare sad smiles, or extract from him any of the lively

41

responses, which once, a short time before, a time hallowed by the memory of his friendship, I had taken for granted. He used to retire into his bedroom and spend hours there, often with the door locked. I would go to cajole and abuse, to say I was sorry and jeer and tease, to beg for his forgiveness and declare that I did not care – he ignored me. Yet his conduct, which I called intolerable, reminded me of mine, which had been more so; and the better part of me recognised the justice of the sentence meted out to its worse accomplice.

Moreover the sulks of James, although they reduced me to charting in my enforced solitude the extent of my transgressions, were never employed as a punitive instrument. They were less a shrewd blow aimed at me, than his spontaneous reaction to the blow that I had dealt him. No idea of revenge seemed to cross his mind, no word of recrimination passed his lips, which, when not tightly compressed, would be simply parted as though to help him to draw into his lungs the fresh recuperative air.

Eventually, after I had implored him for three or four nights in succession to come and have a cigarette in my bedroom, he would surprise me with a smile, a shy herald of that unreserved smile I so longed to see upon his features, and with the faintly humorous remark that he had practically forgotten how to smoke. Trying to conceal my start of joy, I would nonchalantly ask him to fetch a box of matches; and later, from my bed, would again watch the moon illuminate the side of his face, hear his voice regain its normal pitch, and gather by his references not to the past but to what we might do together on the next day, or when we were grown-up, that I had been forgiven.

They lasted, our reconciliations in the moonlight, until my most pressing need of his favour was satisfied. And then the realisation of all I had been through, of the humiliating truth that my young brother had presumed to sit in judgment upon me, was more than enough to arouse my renewed hostility and resentment.

One day displayed every facet of our relations. It was the end of the summer holidays before my last term at school. A travelling circus was coming to a nearby village, and a school friend called Michael Begby, a little older than me, invited me to have lunch and see the show. I accepted with pleasure. But James also wanted to see the circus. And Mama said I could not leave him behind. She would write a note to Mrs Begby and explain the situation. Her interference with my plans, to which I submitted unwillingly, seemed to me another sign of the fond indulgence reserved for her second son.

We set off in the car. Excitement always affected us in different ways – he joked and giggled, while I grew tense and nervous. Although sometimes I enjoyed the mood in which everything amused him, on this occasion, as on the day out shooting, his jokes and laughter jarred, and, by aggravating my anxiety about the impression he would make on my friend Michael, began the recognisable process of exhausting my sympathy. When we arrived at the Begbys', I told the chauffeur who had driven us over not to bother to come and collect us after the circus – there was a fair – we might be late – we would walk the three miles home. I disliked the idea of a long walk home at night, but wished to teach James the lesson that as yet he was not physically equipped to join in my manly enterprises. The fact that he was pleased by the prospect of the walk did not improve my temper.

Mrs Begby, far from being put out by the arrival of an extra guest, as I had promised Mama she would be, read the explanatory note and said she was delighted that I had brought along my brother. At lunch the entire Begby family was charmed by his high spirits, sense of humour, winning manners and insatiable appetite. Because even Michael Begby egged him on, suggesting in an unnaturally deep voice that he should have another bash at the strawberries, I too started to do so, hoping to claim for myself a share of the envied laughter ringing round the table.

But after lunch, on the way to the fairground, Michael was less amused. At length he asked me if I could not 'stop the nipper giggling, for pity's sake!' And my irritation of the morning returned; my latent jealousy, especially of his success with my friends, was defined; and the conflict of loyalties exacerbated my feelings. I tried to draw his attention to Michael's shift of opinion, of which he was blithely unaware, frowned at him and made covert gestures: he continued to play the fool.

We found the circus tent and joined a queue of people waiting to go in. A commissionaire, to whom I felt eternally grateful, insisted on James standing in line behind Michael and me. But all the same I could not attend to Michael's conversation, distracted as I was by anticipation of that one more interruption from my brother, which would give me the opportunity to tell him to damn well shut up. To my surprise he did not interrupt, and after a few minutes I heard not his giggle but a great guffaw of crude laughter, uncomfortably close. I glanced round. For a joke, and against my advice, James had decided to wear one of our father's old tweed caps; it did not fit him and ballooned out over his girlishly long fair hair. Two village youths, next to him in the queue, must have pushed this cap over his eyes, which now looked into mine no longer jokingly or gaily, but with fear and a plea for protection.

I turned back to Michael Begby. A part of me wanted to help my brother – I knew I ought to help him, change his position in the queue or speak sternly to the youths. But I was frightened, did not want to involve Michael in a row, and anyway hoped we would soon be allowed to move into the tent. Besides, and as a matter of fact, I was thrilled by the idea of the retribution overtaking James, and inwardly exclaimed, repeatedly and with relish: it serves him right. I was conscious of a jostling behind me, listened to the coarse vicious taunts and imitations of a girl's refined voice, and again to those alarming guffaws of laughter. But I squared my shoulders and did nothing.

Then my sleeve was gently tugged, and to my ears came the small single cry: 'Fra!'

Without turning my head, in my imagination, I saw the scene perfectly, the piteous aspect of James, the leering faces of his persecutors. My divided heart beat very fast. I began to blush, and felt momentarily paralysed by awful shame and awful joy. It was too late to protect him, my cowardice and resentment assured me – he did not deserve to be protected.

But the hand kept on tugging at my sleeve, and the small cry was reiterated: 'Fra, please!'

Unable to bear any more of it, I gave way to anger, a simplifying anger against all the impossible difficulties of the day, of which he and he alone seemed to be the cause, and swung round on him and said: 'Oh do be quiet!'

The queue began to move. Michael, who appeared to notice nothing, was still talking. James, bullied by the

45

youths, was silent. We paid and took our seats. And slowly, as I stopped being angry, the horrified appreciation of my betrayal outside, the remorse which made it hard for me to meet those shocked yet unaccusing eyes in a strained white face, and the dread that he would sulk, combined to recall or release the affection already welling from its mysterious source the more abundantly for having been checked. I forgot Michael Begby, whom I had never actually liked much, and sat as close as possible to my brother on the rough bench, now and again offering him unselfishly, from a box of chocolates we had bought, the ones with toffee centres of which we were equally fond.

For most of the performance he sat in an attitude I knew well, bent forwards, hugging himself with his arms, shoulders hunched, legs crossed and intertwined. He thanked me in monosyllables for the chocolates and smiled with wistful amusement when I commented on the daring feats of acrobat or lion-tamer. Sometimes he cast at me a puzzled glance, expressive of the unanswerable question: what had he done, what crime apart from that of his happiness had he committed, to merit my brutal repudiation? But he did not sulk. My penitence, as undisguised and heartfelt as the emotions it replaced, may have helped him to gratify more quickly than usual his ever-present wish to forgive me. Towards the end of the performance, after pointing out with a less constrained gesture something or other that caught his fancy, he turned and smiled, as though to say 'Sorry, Fra – it's over now – I'm better – you needn't worry.'

The circus finished. We toured the sideshows. Michael Begby, displeased at no longer receiving from me the dues of deference he counted on, said goodbye and departed. Night had fallen, and by the glare of hurricane lamps, beside a gaudily painted caravan, James and I shared fish and chips in a newspaper cone on which we had spent our last shilling. Then, leaving behind us the smells of cooking, oranges, animals and trodden grass, lingering for a moment by the bright outlying booths, we started to walk home to Lyne.

The sounds of strident churning music, cries of showmen, shots of rifles, and shrieks of girls on the swings receded, or were wafted to us on the purer air of the breeze with a romantic nostalgic faintness. The lights of the fair and within the village began to twinkle fitfully, like the stars up above, far beyond our reach. And the country night, still and solemn, enclosed us, deepening our united mood of an enjoyment straightforward enough, even if it was based on the complex idea of reconciliation.

We ceased to talk merely of the coconut I had won at a shy, or the pennies we had rolled and lost, and in a hushed voice James mentioned the youths in the queue – 'Weren't they terrible, Fra?'

I thought at first he meant to reproach me. But realising his forgiveness was so complete that to his way of thinking there was nothing to forgive, and it had not occurred to him that his reference to the youths might activate my guilt; encouraged by his generosity; liberated by his sincere desire to share more than just the fish and chips with me – once more I let my mind play on the subject of the dark side of myself, which sought to encompass his downfall. I could not understand it. I seemed to be composed of two people, destined never to meet, never to know each other. For the time being I could conceive of no feelings different from those which caused my heart to expand as we walked home under the moon, that moon which in my memory often shone upon our love or hate. Its silver light, in a haunted wood through which our road led, was suddenly extinguished. And although any physical contact between us was becoming a bit awkward, I put my arm round my brother's shoulder, to soothe our common fears of the gloomy wood, to answer without saying anything his question about the youths, to tell him how sorry I was, and assure him that now and for ever afterwards I would be brave and constant in his defence.

Blazer Whitlock

I T WAS THE first day of the autumn term. The boys
were gathered in the twin classrooms known as The
Double-Barrel, discussing the new master. The
school bell rang, a gangway was cleared, a gradual hush
descended, the door from the Private Side banged, voices
were heard. Mr Beaman in a plus-four suit of Harris
tweed passed between the lines of boys, followed by a
man with a brown face, wearing a blue blazer with a
gaudy crest embroidered on the breast pocket.

Mr Beaman made his traditional joke about there being
no need to shoot out of The Double-Barrel, at which the
boys laughed heartily and filed after him into Hall, where
tea was laid on the long deal tables. The new master, Mr
Whitlock, was introduced to the school, grace was said,
and Mr Beaman padded out of the room on his flat feet.
The boys sat down to their slices of corned beef, bread
and a mixture of butter and margarine, raspberry jam
with pips like fine gravel, coconut cakes and weak tea
that tasted of chalk.

Ian Trayle, eleven years old, sat next to his friend
Lidgett. Mr Whitlock strolled amongst the tables, stop-
ping now and again to speak to a boy. When he reached
Ian's table he asked Lidgett his name.

Lidgett replied in his husky voice: 'Lidgett major, sir.'

Mr Whitlock, whose distinct mouth was oddly twisted

49

with embarrassment said: 'You're not related to the Lidgett who was here three years ago?'

'Yes, he's my brother, sir.'

'Then you're Lidgett minor,' said Mr Whitlock, smiling and showing his elongated narrow white teeth.

'No, sir, now my brother's left I'm a major, I'm only called Minor,' Lidgett answered precisely, 'and my minor's called Minimus, though he's really a minor.'

At this Mr Whitlock laughed loudly and easily, losing his taut expression, while Lidgett tried to explain that although he and his younger brother were officially major and minor, they were nicknamed Minor and Minimus in consideration of the fact that they were the second and third Lidgett boys.

When the laughter had subsided Ian asked Mr Whitlock: 'Did you know my brother, sir? He was here three years ago.'

'What was his name?'

'William Trayle, sir.'

'Trayle?' The darkness of the brown eyes was disconcerting. 'You're Trayle's brother?'

'Yes, sir.'

'Well, when you write to him you tell him Blazer Whitlock's back at Beaman's.'

'Blazer, sir?' asked Ian, smiling, but not sure what to make of the new master.

'Yes, Blazer, like this,' said Mr Whitlock, patting the bulging pockets of his blue blazer with smooth brown hands. 'And we'll talk of old Trayler again,' he added, pointing at Ian, as he proceeded farther along the table.

*

Minor and Minimus Lidgett and Ian Trayle shared a room in School Block, so-called because it housed all the classrooms except the Double-Barrel. A wooden partition, rising to within a few feet of the ceiling, divided the room, of which the Lidgett brothers occupied the larger part. The room overlooked the square tarmac yard around which the school was built.

On the first evening of term the three friends, homesick and communicative, unable to settle in their hard beds and chafed by the rough sheets, agreed after the lights were put out that Blazer Whitlock might be a bit funny but was certainly an improvement on Mr Tatton, who had luckily died during the holidays. On the second evening of term they revised their opinion, agreeing he was pretty decent. Four days after his arrival Blazer Whitlock had become the most popular master in the school.

Two incidents in particular contributed to his sudden popularity. One took place on the first Saturday morning after the school had assembled. He was going through the curriculum with the Fifth Classical Form, when a small bird flew into the room and began to flutter against the window and flit about, chirping all the time in a pitiful fashion. Mr Whitlock had the window opened wide, in the hope that the bird would fly out again, and told the boys to sit quietly so as not to frighten it. But the contrary bird settled on the top of a cupboard and refused to move. Mr Whitlock tried to catch it in his mortar-board: the bird squawked and flew to the ledge above the door. He tried again: it flew back to the cupboard. At length a boy called 'Beetle' Henty was sent to fetch his butterfly net. Sitting on Mr Whitlock's shoulders and egged on by the other boys, Henty eventually succeeded in trapping the poor creature. He extracted it from the green net and held it in his hands.

Blazer Whitlock stroked its angry-looking head with a long brown finger, and asked what sort of bird it was.

'I think it's a finch, sir,' Henty replied.

'Take it along to Mr Finch in that case'– Mr Finch was the French master – 'take it along to Mr Finch' – Blazer Whitlock thought for a moment, his mouth twisted to one side in a sly smile – 'and say: Mr Whitlock's compliments and is this finch any relation?'

'Say that?' 'Beetle' Henty gaped.

'Yes, sir, say that, sir, and say sir, sir. All right?'

'Yes, sir,' said Henty, looking puzzled and unhappy.

The rest of the form awaited his return with impatience.

Mr Whitlock shut the windows, sat down at his desk, spoke calmly again of the term's curriculum.

He seemed not to notice when Henty reappeared, allowing the boy to stand uncomfortably at his side, until he turned to him and said: 'What have you done with that bird?'

'I've given it to Mr Finch, sir.'

'You've given Mr Finch the bird?'

'Yes, sir.'

Mr Whitlock laughed in his wild unexpected way.

'No, sir,' Henty corrected himself, slapping his hands against his thighs and joining in the general laughter.

'What did you say to Mr Finch?'

'I said, sir – Mr Whitlock's compliments, sir, and is this finch any relation?'

'And what did Mr Finch say?'

'He said, sir – thank Mr Whitlock and tell him, yes, it's my uncle.'

The second incident took place on the Sunday evening. The school was congregated in The Cavern, a large wooden recreation room adjoining the main buildings. Somebody had heard that for the last three years Mr Whitlock had been teaching in India, and when he came on duty a group of boys began to question him. Yes, he admitted, sitting on the steps of the dais at the end of the room, he had left Beaman's School to join the staff of the Mysore Academy. What was India like, he was asked.

His face shadowed by the lights that hung from the high rafters, one knee raised and clasped by his linked brown fingers, Blazer Whitlock described it. Boys got up from the tables ranged round the walls and stood at the edge of the group. Games and stamp albums were deserted. Soon the whole school clustered about the dais, listening to tales of fakirs and beds of nails, of the Temple of the Tooth and the Taj Mahal, of snake-charmers and funeral pyres, told in a voice that never rose above a certain level but managed to impart to every sentence strange gripping hints of the alien and the macabre.

For an hour he spoke of Indian life and Indian customs. That hour, and the business with the bird, provided the boys with a sort of reference. Afterwards they knew why Blazer Whitlock was more than pretty decent, they were confirmed in their opinion of his decency, they could recall his story of the cobra under the lavatory seat, convinced that no other master possessed such a wide experience, was so interesting, so entertaining and unique.

The attributes that really drew them together they sensed but were unable to express. They sensed for instance that with them he felt at ease, he could talk freely, whereas with the other masters he would employ a tone of almost angry deference, twisting his mouth into a travesty of a smile, blinking his eyes, and jerking back his head and shoulders. They recognised his preference for their company; relished his wild laughter, and respected his laughing – without superiority or sarcasm – at what did not amuse them; they appreciated his eccentricity, his talent for entirely forgetting himself – one afternoon he rolled his trousers over his knees, took off his shoes, and performed an Indian dance in his Fair Isle socks; and they were thrilled by his stories for the best of reasons, because he was thrilled by them too. Moreover their sympathy had a physical basis. They liked to throw their arms round the neck of this middle-aged man with the short grizzled hair, they did not wriggle away when he tickled them, and they disputed for the pleasure of leaning heavily against him when he sat on the dais in The Cavern, telling his stories.

Inevitably, an element in the school mistook all the freedom for licence. A week after the term began this tendency was sharply corrected.

Mr Whitlock had been working with the Fifth Classical Form. There were a few minutes left before lunch, and somebody knocked on the door and was told to come in. A boy called Theobald entered. Theobold was nearly six feet tall, gangling and lax, with a high-pitched voice and a silly giggle, and was the only boy in the school to possess a solid gold pencil. He giggled as he walked between the desks towards the master's rostrum, and he giggled in the pause that ensued after he had reached it.

'Please, sir,' he began at last, lisping slightly.

Mr Whitlock, sitting at his desk and resting his forehead against his hand, interrupted him without looking up.

'Go out of the room and come in properly,' he said.

Theobald turned with another giggle and a faint shrug of his shoulders, and left the room, swinging his arms in a limp disjointed fashion.

A boy laughed, the lunch bell rang, another boy began to pile his books together noisily, and Theobald knocked again on the door.

'Who's collecting his books?' asked Mr Whitlock, still without looking up.

Henty grinned sheepishly and said: 'Me, sir.'

'Who is me? Stand up, that boy.'

Henty rose to his feet and Theobald knocked on the door.

'Why did you collect your books?'

'Well, sir, the bell . . .'

'This division is not over until I dismiss you. Open your books.'

'Yes, sir. May I sit down, sir?'

'No, you may not.'

There was now a rather tense silence in the classroom. Theobald thumped on the door, seemingly with the flat of his hand, making it rattle. Mr Whitlock did not move or speak. Theobald was heard to giggle. The boys waited uncertainly, some smiling, some afraid they would be kept late, some nervous.

Theobald knocked more politely on the door.

Again he approached the rostrum.

'Well?' enquired Mr Whitlock quietly, lowering his hand and standing up. His face was paler than usual and his eyes swimmingly black.

'Mr Finch's compliments, sir' – Theobald accentuated the sir – 'and I'm to tell you what I said. We were translating French, sir, and we came to "Go to the devil" – that was the English, sir – and I said, "Allez au Blazer."'

There was a pause, then Theobald giggled loosely. None of the other boys laughed.

'What does that mean?' Mr Whitlock asked, blinking and obviously angry.

'Well, sir, I meant "Go to blazes . . ." It was a joke, sir.'

'I see.'

Theobald, apparently grasping the situation, said: 'I'm sorry, sir.'

'What am I supposed to do?'

'Mr Finch said, sir, please would you punish me.'

'Don't do it again. Now get out, all get out!' snapped Mr Whitlock, turning and starting to wipe the blackboard with a wet duster.

'Oh merci *bonko*!' said Theobald, giggling at his variation of merci beaucoup.

Mr Whitlock whirled round, his eyes absolutely flashing, and repeated to Theobald several times, 'What did you say? What did you say?' in a furious voice.

The other boys were standing, gathering their books, talking and moving towards the door. They stopped and turned.

'Merci *bonko*,' stammered Theobald.

Mr Whitlock struck him a frightful blow on the head.

He screamed and staggered to one side. The master rushed from the room, swearing terribly under his breath.

Ian Trayle was a member of the Fifth Classical Form. He was therefore present both when the finch was caught and when Theobald was hit on the head. Mr Whitlock's violence impressed him deeply. The other masters were often angry, but then Mr Beaman would shout and award extra lines; Mr Finch would tweak at hair, though once he had shaken Minor Lidgett like a rat; Mr Hyde the padre would glare reproachfully out of his sunken eyes and punish whole forms at a time. None of them had ever lost his temper so completely as Blazer Whitlock lost his, and none of them had ever bashed a boy. And although Ian was afraid of Mr Beaman, who wielded the power of ultimate punishment – a beating with one of his huge gym-shoes – and also of Mr Hyde's icy sarcasm and the collective sentences for wrongdoing imposed with a gentle curling smile, his fear of the anger of neither of these masters compared with the emotions which Blazer Whitlock had inspired.

He could not forget the scene. He could not forget the whiteness of the master's usually brown face, or the eastern darkness of his eyes, or the snapping up and down of his eyelids, or the furious repetition of the question 'What did you say?' – or the cracking sound of the blow, or Theobald's scream, or Mr Whitlock's exit from the room, the flapping of his black gown and the mutter of dire swearwords.

After the master had gone, Ian became conscious of the fact that he was blushing, that he burnt with the heat of fear and a sort of shame, and that his hair seemed to be standing on end. He joined the boys surrounding Theobald, who was blubbering and vowing he would write to his father. He raised his voice in the chorus of sympathy, although before the blow was delivered he himself had felt angry with Theobald. And then, at lunch, he described the scene to Minor Lidgett.

'He said "Merci *bonko*"?' Minor asked incredulously. 'What happened next?'

'Blazer hit him.'

'What with?'

'His hand, his fist.'

'Where?'

'On the ear.'

'How hard did he hit him?'

'As hard as he could.'

'And what did Theobald do?'

'He screamed.'

'Screamed?'

'Yes, screamed.'

'Theobald's soft. I think he deserved it.'

'But Minor, it was a terrific wallop. And Blazer lost his bait, his face got all funny and things.'

'It was jolly decent of Blazer not to punish him for saying "Allez au Blazer". Theobald's so sloppy. And then "Merci *bonko*"! He might have got beaten.'

'Yes, I know. But you weren't there.'

Ian did not argue with Minor, whose opinion was soon shared by the rest of the school. He even accepted his view. But thereafter, whenever a stupid or impertinent remark was made in the Fifth Classical, when anyone went too far with Blazer Whitlock, he would feel a tightening of his nerves and would search the master's face, to see whether he had changed colour or was blinking.

Ian Trayle was a member of the group which had begun the questioning of Mr Whitlock on the first Sunday evening of term. This group consisted of the Lidgett brothers, the fat boy 'Egg' Hampton, and Denis Preston, who was twelve years old, tall and muscular. Although not quite at the top of the school, the five of them were enterprising and closely-knit, and together wielded more power amongst the other boys than their individual positions merited. And they became the particular supporters and associates of the new master.

On Sundays, and the Wednesday and Saturday half-holidays, they would seek him out when he came on duty. In the mild October weather, free afternoons were spent on the playing field. There, the middle-aged man and his young friends would find a secluded sunlit spot and throw themselves down on the warm cropped grass. The cries of footballers would reach them. A tennis ball would drop out of the pale blue sky, roll amongst them and be returned. They would suck grasses, watch the flight of a model aeroplane, Blazer Whitlock reclining on an elbow and applying his lighter to the black bowl of his pipe for the tenth time. As the days grew shorter and colder, one of the friends would commandeer the right to pair with him on school walks, another would claim him for a partner in card games, a third would try to reserve a place beside him when he told his stories in The Cavern.

Four weeks passed.

It was a wet Saturday afternoon and the boys had been

playing in the tarmac yard. They were gathering their coats from the pegs on the wall and streaming through the swing-doors to get ready for tea. Blazer Whitlock called to Ian – he was putting on his blazer.

Ian ran across, jumped and landed with a thump before him, laughed and enquired: 'Yes, sir?'

'I want to talk to you,' said Mr Whitlock.

Ian studied his face – he was looking away, but smiling, and his words surely contained more a humorous than an ominous ring.

'Talk to me, sir?'

Mr Whitlock shouted at a boy whose wallet had fallen out of his coat pocket.

'Yes.' He turned and gazed at Ian, suddenly averting his eyes. 'When could you come to my classroom?'

He had produced his pipe and tobacco-pouch, and now began to knock the pipe against the palm of his hand and run his little finger round the inside of the bowl.

'When would you like?' asked Ian, watching him.

'What time do you go to bed?'

'About seven, sir.'

'Come and see me then.' Mr Whitlock looked up and smiled. 'Could you?'

'Yes, of course, sir.'

'Good.'

The master spoke lightly, finally, smiling again and putting his pipe in his mouth.

But Ian asked: 'Sir, what's it about?'

'Nothing. You'll find out.'

'What is it, sir?' he insisted, laughing.

'Nothing.'

'But it is, sir. Do tell me.'

60

'No, it's not.'

Mr Whitlock's smile became a trifle pained. The joke of 'You'll find out' was no longer amusing. He held his pipe in his hand and queried: 'Seven o'clock?'

Ian answered: 'Yes, sir,' and went indoors.

He grew increasingly apprehensive as the evening progressed. He had never appeared before a master out of school hours, except in order to be punished. There were no crimes on his conscience, nevertheless he felt guilty. He also felt afraid. He remembered Mr Whitlock's strange diffidence and the way he had cut his laughter short. He repeated to himself the assurance that it was nothing; but then, he wondered, what was it, and what would it lead to? Because he was ashamed of his fear, which his reason told him was groundless, he did not mention his appointment to Minor Lidgett or anyone. At seven o'clock, trembling slightly, he knocked on the dark door of the classroom.

He was told to come in.

Mr Whitlock was sitting not at his desk on the rostrum, but at one of the boys' desks. He glanced over his shoulder as Ian entered, and said: 'Shut the door and come up here.' Then he turned back to the papers which were scattered in front of him, placed his elbows on the desk and rested his forehead in his hands.

Ian closed the door and, without speaking, walked between the rows of desks on his left and the cream-coloured wall on his right. At the end of the gangway, in the space between the desks and the rostrum, he stopped and stood with his hands at his sides.

Mr Whitlock said to him: 'Did you tell everyone you were coming to see me?'

'No, sir.'

'Who did you tell?'

'Nobody, sir.'

'But you came across with Lidgett?'

'Came across, sir?'

'To go to bed.'

'No, I came by myself.'

'These are your Latin verses.'

'Yes, sir.'

'I've been correcting them . . .'

Throughout this conversation Mr Whitlock remained in the same position, his forehead resting in his hands, the little fingers pointing outwards. Light from the bare bulb with its white china shade fell on his neck, his stiff short hair, his smooth hands and round silver wristwatch with large luminous figures.

'I've been correcting them,' he repeated, and lowering a hand he shifted a piece of paper.

'Yes, sir?' Ian enquired, his heart beating noticeably.

Mr Whitlock looked round and said: 'They're all right.'

'Are they?' Ian exclaimed, smiling with relief. 'Are they, sir?' And now he noticed that his legs felt weak.

'Did you think I asked you here to give you a berry?'

'No, sir,' Ian lied.

'Don't call me sir and I bet you did.'

'No, sir – I mean, yes – well . . . I wasn't sure, sir,' Ian laughed. 'I wasn't sure.'

'I wouldn't give you a berry, Trayler,' Mr Whitlock said in a gentle voice, twisting his mouth slightly to one side. 'Don't worry. Sit down.'

'Thank you, sir.'

'Not sir,' said Mr Whitlock very gently indeed.

'Well . . .' Ian began, meaning: well, what am I to call you?

Mr Whitlock replied: 'You can call me Blazer if you like,' and began to fill his pipe.

He and Ian were sitting at adjoining desks. The boy had lost his fear and was already accepting the peculiarity of the situation. He had often stayed behind to talk to a master after some division, and these moments with Mr Whitlock – with Blazer – were not so different. He did not call other masters by their nicknames, but then Blazer was not like other masters. He smiled at his anxiety, the removal of which disposed him to feel grateful and especially friendly, and thought of the diverting tale he would soon be able to tell Minor and Minimus Lidgett.

But Blazer Whitlock reached into his pocket and said carelessly: 'Do you eat that stuff?' – and tossed a bar of milk chocolate onto Ian's desk.

'Gosh,' Ian breathed, round-eyed with longing and astonishment, for chocolate and sweets were absolutely not allowed, were considered to be punishable contraband, at Beaman's School.

'Eat it here.'

'Now?'

'Go on.'

'What about you?'

Ian raised his eyes, and Blazer Whitlock gazed into them, shook his head, smiled and repeated: 'Go on.'

'Are you certain you won't have some?'

'Yes.'

'Thanks awfully!'

Ian broke the chocolate and put two pieces into his mouth.

63

'Do you like it?'

'I love it, it's my favourite kind.'

'Have another bit.'

'Can I eat it all?'

'Will you be sick?'

'Oh sir!'

'Not sir, Trayler.'

'Oh, sorry.'

Blazer Whitlock lit his pipe and Ian munched at the crisp and creamy chocolate until his jaws ached and he had to pause for breath.

'Is it fun, correcting Latin verses?' he asked, leaning across, sucking his teeth and swallowing.

'Not exactly . . . Put that away if anyone comes in.'

'I'll put it in this pocket.'

'And remember, we're working.'

'What are we working at?' Ian asked with an excited giggle.

'You're working on the chocolate,' Blazer smiled.

'I wish work was always like this.'

'So do I. But remember.'

'All right,' Ian agreed, giggling again and eating more of the chocolate. Blazer Whitlock puffed at his pipe. 'Do you like being back at Beaman's?'

'Yes, Trayler, yes, I do.'

'Where are the other masters now?'

'Probably in the common-room.'

'What'll they be doing?'

'Oh, sitting about and talking.'

'Don't you sit with them?'

Blazer blinked. 'I'm perfectly happy here. Is the chocolate good?'

'It's delicious.'

'What's that?'

Steps resounded in the concrete passage. Mr Whitlock took the pipe out of his mouth and signalled to Ian with a frown to pocket the chocolate. Ian did so, and chewed, swallowed and choked slightly. They listened, not moving. A strained unnatural expression had appeared on the master's face. Blue smoke rose silently from his pipe, and the steps passed by.

After a pause Ian whispered: 'That was Mr Hyde.'

'Finish the chocolate,' Blazer whispered back.

Ian put the remaining two pieces in his mouth.

'What about the paper?'

'Give it to me.'

'What's the time, sir?'

Abruptly the master looked down at the papers.

Blushing, Ian said aloud: 'Oh dear, I keep forgetting.'

'Try not to. Try and remember – Blazer – will you?'

'Yes, of course, of course I will.'

Blazer stood up and edged out from behind the desk. Once more he smiled at Ian. But the boy felt an unaccountable ache of sadness.

'I'm awfully sorry,' he said, standing too.

'What for?'

He could not explain. All at once he was sad for a multitude of reasons: because he could not remember to call Blazer by his nickname, because he was at school. He recalled that the term was not half gone; for months he would have to sit in classrooms, run along clammy corridors, inhale the dusty smell of chalk, the acrid smell of ink, the cloying smell of cabbage. Liberty was a lifetime away and home hardly even a hope. He looked up at the odd kind man with his uneasy smile and brown face, and felt sorry both for Blazer and for himself.

He thanked him for the chocolate.

'It wasn't too much, was it?' the master asked, removing his pipe and putting his hand on Ian's shoulder.

'No! Once I ate four bars running.'

They laughed.

'Don't say anything about tonight.'

'No.'

'Come and see me again sometimes, in the evenings.'

'Yes, I will.'

'Good night, Trayler.'

Blazer patted Ian's shoulder, kissed him on the forehead, then turned hurriedly and replaced his pipe in his mouth.

Ian blushed again, said 'Good night, Blazer,' and left the room.

Ian Trayle kept his visit to Blazer Whitlock's classroom a secret because of the forbidden bar of chocolate, and because he had been asked to say nothing. But anyway he could not have spoken of the experience.

Ian had been at Beaman's School for two years. Everyone there had been quite kind to him: Mr Beaman often asked how he was getting on, and he was not bullied. Yet his home and his mother and father were far away, and his brother William was at public school.

He had adapted to his new life. His first term at Beaman's created an altered but adequate Ian, who was never too hopeful or too despondent, too vulnerable, too incautious. In the holidays, he had assured himself, he would let himself go and recapture the happiness and excitement of the golden age of his childhood.

Eventually the holidays arrived, and he recaptured nothing. He had a good time, but it was different. He could not or would not abandon his reserve.

Little by little, in the course of the two years or six terms, the Ian Trayle of the Fifth Classical Form and his group of school friends seemed to become the real Ian, while the Ian who was so close to his mother, who looked up to his father and hero-worshipped William, became a creature almost of fantasy, ridiculously sensitive and enthusiastic and moody, and recollected with a mixture of condescension and scorn.

Blazer Whitlock changed things again. Ian on that autumn evening entered the classroom admiring, fearing and rather liking the master. The realisation that a grown-up invested with the power of worldwide experience, physical strength, position and popularity was reversing the natural order to the extent of suing for his favours startled and displeased him. He wanted to co-operate before he was asked to do so, and thus salve Blazer's pride for his own peace of mind. But in order to anticipate wishes, he had to take a closer look at the person who was wishing; the result was that he recognised in Blazer's evasive black eyes the sadness and loneliness he had forsworn and hidden in himself.

The exchange in the classroom brought to light unsettling emotions in the boy as well as the master. Or perhaps Blazer played upon the native empathy of Ian. Anyway, the latter could no longer deny his nostalgia for the old days. He regretted the loss of liberty to care with all his heart. He was forced to admit that he hated school, and the necessity of concealing his feelings, and expedient associations instead of loving ones, and irrelevant lessons in place of private passionate labour.

For these unconventional reasons Ian was pleased to keep Blazer's secret. As for the kiss, it was merely another of the embarrassments of the evening.

The term wore on.

Although Ian was occasionally sadder and more homesick than before, he was also more receptive and aware, and might have been happier, but for Blazer Whitlock.

Twice or three times a week Blazer would keep him back after a division, or detain him on the playing-field, or call to him in the yard, and ask him to look in on his way to bed. And Ian would have to detach himself from his companions at seven o'clock and slip across to the classroom, which he entered more boldly, without bothering to knock on the door.

Once he burst in, laughing, and found Mr Hyde warming his hands in front of the fire. The padre turned a round-eyed disapproving gaze upon him, then glanced interrogatively at his colleague, who looked pale and wild. Ian was ordered to go out and knock, and was kept waiting until Mr Hyde, softly and curiously smiling, had taken his leave. Blazer was obviously distressed by this occurrence, but he did not and Ian dared not refer to it.

In spite of the freedom that the school, and the group of friends, enjoyed in the presence of Blazer, Ian, alone with him, never felt free. He was always on guard, anxious in case he should hurt Blazer, provoke one of his abasing appeals, or in the last resort fire his temper. He had to be ready to cover modestly, to dress, the raw wounds which the master seemed to long to lay bare.

His attempts to avoid responsibility were a responsibility in themselves.

Yet it did not occur to Ian to refuse to see Blazer Whitlock in the evenings. He respected Blazer's authority: in fact, longed to maintain it. And he knew that if he ever got to the classroom late, or left it too soon, Blazer would lower his eyes abruptly, smile crookedly, tell him it did not matter in his gentlest voice, and that he must not worry. He had neither the heart nor the nerve to refuse anything, to bear either the other's or his own complementary sadness, or utter tongue-tied excuses which would not be believed and might infuriate.

So he complied, he accepted every invitation, arriving punctually and waiting as patiently as possible for his dismissal.

He was frequently bored by Blazer. That he was uncertain, until he entered the classroom, of how he would be greeted, added a not altogether welcome piquancy to his visits. Sometimes the master played practical jokes on him, hiding under a desk or balancing books on the top of the door. One evening he and the boy tried to climb round the room without touching the floor. But such active and amusing times were rare. Usually Blazer was quiet, melancholy, and then Ian would ask innumerable questions, loll restlessly on a desk or against the mantelpiece, estimate his chances of receiving a bar of chocolate, despising himself for his materialistic hope – and feel shifty when it was fulfilled, cross when it was not.

Ian was never easy in his mind about the chocolate, because he looked forward to it more than to the company of the giver, because it was a sort of bribe, and because it created a rift of injustice between himself and Minor and Minimus Lidgett.

The Lidgett brothers noticed his tendency to disappear in the evenings, and asked questions which he had to parry or answer with lies. After a few weeks of it, he capitulated and confessed that he was seeing Mr Whitlock.

'But what for?' Minor queried.

'Well, just to talk.'

'What does he want to talk about?'

'Oh, things.'

'Blazer's funny,' Minor observed, not very originally, shaking his head.

'Yes, he is,' Ian agreed, glad to be able to dissociate himself from the master's funniness, whilst at the same time feeling disloyal and ungrateful.

He warned Minor and Minimus not to broadcast the news.

'What's so secret?'

'You know what Blazer's like.'

One evening soon afterwards, in the classroom, Ian paused in the middle of munching chocolate to say: 'Blazer, could I take a bit of this up to Minor and Minimus?'

'Do they know you come here? Have you told them?'

'No! But they're bound to find out, they've probably guessed, sharing a room with me. And they'd give me a bit of chocolate if they had it.'

'I don't want the whole school to know.'

'Minor and Minimus wouldn't say a word.'

'There'll be no more chocolate if they do.'

Later, upstairs, Ian lobbed the chocolate over the partition onto Minimus Lidgett's bed.

'What's this?'

'It's chocs, my lad.'

'Where did you get it?'

'With love from Blazer.'

'Golly, good old Blazer!'

The next day, privately and politely, the brothers thanked Mr Whitlock; and on that and future evenings round about seven o'clock were apt to badger Ian to keep his appointments.

Three weeks before the end of the term Ian's mother came down to see him.

She enquired about the new master.

'Is he nice?'

'Yes.'

'Do you like him?'

'Yes.'

'Not much, darling?'

'Yes, I do, Mummy – he's decent.'

But in truth Ian's relationship with Blazer, the pleas and threats and good night kisses, and even the chocolate or its implications, had become impossibly burdensome.

During these final weeks before the Christmas holidays, Blazer was extremely moody. The general attitude towards him had altered. He was still popular, his stories could still enthral; but the traits that had established his popularity undermined it. The boys considered that his clowning, his actions and reactions were too like their own. The fearful fascinating novelty of his capacity for violence wore off, since he did not strike anyone after Theobald. Invariably the prefix 'old' was tacked on to his nickname. When he got irritable, or was gloomy or played the fool, the judgment of the school resolved itself into the formula: 'Old Blazer's at it again, typical of old Blazer.' Sometimes more in favour, sometimes less, and perhaps more laughed at than laughed with, on the whole he was simply taken for granted.

On the afternoon of the very last day of the term the school was assembled in The Cavern. Trials were over, prizes had been distributed, the great high-tea known as The Feast would begin in an hour, followed by The Rag and then The Sing-song. The boys had given themselves up to their excitement. They screamed, romped, tussled and joked, forgot quarrels and invented new ones, and, recollecting the opening words of Mr Beaman's end of term song: 'No more Beaman's, no more school . . .' they bellowed at one another: 'No more chapel, no more work, no more games, no more nothing!'

Blazer Whitlock was on duty. He sat on a wooden armchair on the dais, and the hanging lights seemed to suspend inky shadows from his eyebrows, cheekbones, nose and lower lip.

Ian, pursued by Minor Lidgett, bounded up the steps of the dais and spoke to him, swinging on the arm of his chair.

'Are you going to tell a story tonight at The Sing-song?'
Blazer admitted that he was.
'A frightening one?'
'Maybe.'
'Will you tell us one now?' asked Minor.
'No.'
'No? Why no, sir?' Minor asked for a joke.
'Because I say no.'
'But it is the end of the term!'
'I can hear that.'

'Stop it, Minor,' said Ian, who was being tickled. 'What are you reading?' he asked the master.

'A book.'

'Minor!' cried Ian, making a dive at his escaping friend.

Blazer caught him by the wrist and said in an undertone: 'Trayler, come and see me after The Feast.'

'I'll teach you, Minor!' Ian shouted.

'After The Feast.'

'Oh but it's The Rag then!'

'Just for a minute.'

'But I can't – it's The Rag!'

'I won't see you again.'

'Oh all right. Please let me go. Please!'

Ian tore himself away and fought with Lidgett. They were rolling about under the piano when they heard Blazer Whitlock's voice. It was raised in anger. In The Cavern it rang out above the noise, which rapidly decreased. Minor exclaimed 'Watch it!' – and giggled.

But Ian blushed, his scalp pricked, he crawled from under the piano and struggled to his feet.

The scene was being enacted on the dais. Blazer was standing up, facing a boy, concealing a boy behind his aggressively hunched shoulders.

Other boys in the vicinity were retreating in various directions, some creeping into the body of the room, some pressing back like frightened animals. One stumbled. His feet clattered on the boards, drowning the first words of a question Blazer was asking.

'. . . Or did I not tell you to close the windows?'

The end of the question reverberated in the absolute silence that now prevailed.

'Yes, you did . . .'

'Call me sir!'

Denis Preston had answered. Ian's heart sank. He remembered having seen Denis playing with the windows.

Blazer moved slightly, revealing Denis with a sashcord in his hand, which he swung in an awkward movement from side to side. He looked trapped, and because he was large and strong the impropriety of his present position was accentuated.

Blazer must not lose his temper with Denis, not with my friend, not with his friend, Ian prayed; he must leave Denis alone.

'Yes, you did, sir – you did, sir – but I was closing . . .'

'Don't you argue with me!'

'I'm not –'

Blazer hit him. It all happened very quickly. He raised his hand, in which he still held his book, a finger marking his place, and slapped it down on Denis' face. There was a thud. Denis dropped the sashcord, put his hand to his eye and doubled up with a swift mechanical movement.

'Will that teach you a lesson? Will it?' demanded Blazer Whitlock.

And he seized Denis by the scruff of his jacket, and in a flurry of confused and clumsy activity pushed him down the steps. Denis tripped but righted himself. A shocked mutter arose from the boys, who made way for him. He turned, his hand over one eye, glaring at Blazer with the other, and retired into the crowd. The master began to pace with enormous strides to and fro on the dais, casting black incoherent glances after him.

Minor Lidgett approached Denis, and Minimus Lidgett, Egg Hampton and Ian followed. When Denis removed his hand a small graze on the temple, white in the centre of an already swelling bruise, was discernible.

He said that if Blazer Whitlock put in an appearance at The Rag he would kill him. The group of friends agreed to help. Mr Hyde had come on duty. The school bell rang for The Feast.

Ian ate little of the heavy meal. He in his turn was too angry. Blazer's display of violence had again impressed him. Yet that Denis Preston, a member of the group of friends not only of Ian but of Blazer Whitlock himself, should have been the victim of such an undeserved assault, and on this of all days, filled him with anger to the exclusion of fear. He could not shed his sense of responsibility for events. He felt he had been betrayed, humiliated publicly. The forcible division of his loyalties enraged him. Minor Lidgett and the others began to joke about the imminent assassination of the master; there was laughter, in which even Denis joined; but Ian could not laugh. For the bruised eyebrow, for all the sore spots resulting from the strain of the relationship with which he had been saddled, he was determined to exact a full revenge.

He was trembling, as on the occasion of his first visit, though for different reasons, when he knocked on the classroom door.

'Come in.'

The culprit and criminal in blue blazer and uncreased grey flannels stood on the rostrum, to one side of his desk, in a tense position, almost as if he himself were awaiting a blow.

Colour flooded into his face at the sight of Ian, and he smiled with pleasure.

Through his shining smile he said: 'I thought you wouldn't come.'

Ian, disconcerted, shut the door. The flames of his anger, his imaginary scorching phrases, were damped. He asked 'Why?' in a flat inflexible voice. But somehow the life had gone out of his intended protest.

'No reason, Trayler,' the master replied blandly, still smiling, but slyly now, as if he had produced in an argument some unanswerable proposition. He tapped his pipe against the desk and observed: 'There's The Rag, isn't there? You'll want to get along to that.'

The uproar in The Cavern, where The Rag was beginning, was clearly audible. It reminded Ian that the long term was at an end, and he suffered a shock of happiness. He wanted not to think, not to talk, only to shout and laugh with the other boys. Life was hurrying by, he reflected, while he was confined as usual in the classroom, in a backwater of silence and difficulty. Oh come on, he cried within himself. It did not matter any more that Blazer had struck Denis, or that Blazer had interpreted his – Ian's – presence as a sign of forgiveness. He ached and pined for one thing, just to get away.

Yet he declared contrarily, perhaps because he was so impatient that he scarcely knew what he was saying: 'I don't mind about The Rag.'

'Don't you?' asked Blazer with his vivid smile, obviously surprised.

Why can't you understand? – That's all I do mind about, you damn fool, Ian thought.

Aloud he said: 'Not for a minute.' He expected Blazer to blanch at his violent tone. But the master again misunderstood, he looked delighted, and stuck his pipe in his mouth and blew through it. The familiar whistling and gurgling sound grated on Ian's nerves beyond bearing.

'Perhaps I will go,' he said in a rush. 'Denis and the group are waiting for me.'

'Oh no, please don't do that,' Blazer replied, removing his pipe.

'Yes –' Ian continued excitedly.

He was interrupted.

'No, Trayler, wait.'

'But I really can't, I really must –'

'No, Trayler –'

'Yes –'

'Will you shut up and come here!'

Blazer had stepped off the rostrum. His face was white and his black eyes blinked and flashed.

Will he hit me, Ian wondered. He shook all over from the beating of his heart. Let him, he thought, let him hit me!

But instead of hitting Ian, Blazer stopped, his mouth opened, he tried to smile or laugh, twisting his sharply defined purplish lips away from his elongated teeth, and then jerked out: 'Sorry, Trayler, I didn't mean to speak like that. But you mustn't go for a minute – I shan't see you . . .' He lowered his eyes. 'If you hang on, I'll come to The Rag – I want to have a word with Denis.'

'All right.'

'Is it all right?' Blazer managed to laugh at the back of his throat and through his nose. 'I wouldn't get cross with you, Trayler.'

'No,' Ian smiled, but he thought: you did.

'Sorry,' Blazer said again, sitting down, slumping down at one of the desks.

Ian, standing behind him, realised vaguely he had won the day. At least he had extracted the promise of some sort of overture, perhaps an apology, to Denis. But noticing Blazer's bowed head, and his hands fiddling shakily with his rolled leather tobacco-pouch and empty pipe, he was afraid that his victory had not set him free.

He began: 'Blazer –'

'Yes?'

'Are you going home tomorrow?'

'Yes, I am.'

'Are you looking forward to it?'

'No. No, I'm not. You go home too?'

'Yes.'

'Remember me to your brother . . . Where are you?'

'Here.'

Ian moved along the gangway.

Blazer asked as he filled his pipe with the curls of dark damp tobacco: 'I suppose you'd like the holidays to last for ever?'

'Yes, I would.'

'Will you forget what I said, Trayler?'

Ian queried, caught unawares: 'What?'

'Forget what I said.'

'Oh yes.'

Blazer rose to his feet, dusting the tobacco from his trousers, muttered something about a mistake, and turned to the boy. His face had regained its brown colour, but the skin round the mouth and chin seemed to hang in folds. He remarked, not quite with a sneer: 'But I'm keeping you, aren't I?'

'No.'

'One minute more . . .' He gazed at Ian, then swivelled, placed his elbow on the desk on the rostrum, leant his head on his hand and exclaimed: 'Oh Trayler!'

'But it's all right,' Ian insisted, hoping to reassure, to

78

get it over, to have done with it once and for ever, but thinking: this is terrible.

'I'll write to you,' Blazer said. 'Do you like letters?'

'Yes.'

'But not answering – not answering letters?'

'No.'

Blazer fished his lighter out of his pocket.

'You'll drop a line though?'

'Yes, I will.'

'Cross your heart?'

'Yes, of course.'

'We'd better go.'

Having lit his pipe, Blazer laid a hand on Ian's shoulder and said: 'Thanks for coming this evening.'

'Blazer, you will tell Denis . . . Won't you?'

'Yes.'

They avoided each other's eyes.

'Don't hold – I mean, you have forgotten, Trayler?'

'Yes.'

'Goodbye, my dear creature.'

He kissed Ian lengthily and very tenderly on the forehead.

'Goodbye,' Ian replied, feeling troubled and sad through his relief.

The Rag was nearly over and the boys were taking their places round the piano. Miss Flynn the music mistress struck several chords for Mr Finch, who performed imitations on his cello of a bumble-bee and a bus going up a hill. He was made to repeat the latter three times. Then Miss Flynn played chopsticks, Mr Hyde told a whimsical

79

story about a train that lost its way, and Mr Beaman sang his end of term song.

Ian sat with the group of friends. Every so often he became conscious of the fact that Blazer, standing on the far side of the piano, was watching him – and responded with a frank smile, refusing to meet or satisfy the demands in those intense dark eyes. He sensed it was cruel of him not to smile lingeringly, not to issue the messages of absolution and secret cheer that Blazer seemed to desire; but he did not want to separate himself from the justly joyous mood of the rest of the school, or to be reminded of the recent scene in the classroom. He resented the master's pleading and mournful glances, and even took a certain pleasure in denying them.

For his troubled feeling persisted; only with an effort could he put it from him. His victory in the classroom, he now realised, had clarified nothing. The declared object of his visit had been achieved – Blazer had undertaken to speak to Denis Preston. Moreover Ian had made Blazer pay for his conduct towards Denis, Theobald, other boys and himself, for having inspired fear, for having inspired boredom, and so on. He had vented his accumulated wrath. But the underlying object of the whole exercise, to resolve the misunderstandings, to remove the misapprehensions of his personal situation, was farther than ever from achievement. He had gained his victory not by telling Blazer the truth, that he wished to have no more private dealings with him, but by a trick, because he had provoked Blazer to lose his temper. And as victor on such a basis he had felt that he had to pretend to an affection, and in a heightened form, which he had come to the classroom to disclaim. His situation was not better, it was worse. He had really been defeated.

Blazer's story was the concluding item of the evening's entertainment. Miss Flynn and the masters had left The Cavern, the boys had rearranged themselves into a semi-circle round the dying coal fire, in front of which the brown-faced man puffed at his pipe, warming his hands behind his back. Before he began he called for Denis Preston.

Denis, sitting beside Ian, answered: 'Here, sir.'

'Turn out the lights, Denis,' Blazer said in a friendly voice. Then suddenly he shouted: 'Unless you want another black eye!'

The school burst into laughter.

'Boys are not allowed to leave Beaman's School wearing one shoe, one sock, or one black eye. Come here, Denis.'

The school was convulsed with laughter. Denis, joining in the general mirth, switched out the lights.

'Come here.'

Denis stepped into the ring of squatting and reclining boys.

'Do you expect me to give you another black eye, two lovely black eyes?' Blazer laughed his former wild, flowing and infectious laugh. 'Well, you're not going to get it – sorry. Sit down, old dunghill. Now!'

Denis returned to his place beside Ian. The laughter subsided. Blazer sat on the wooden armchair.

'Now, you wanted me to tell you a story, I believe,' he said. 'There is a story, a true story, I think it might amuse you to hear. But I warn you, it's not a pretty tale. Perhaps a few of you, anyone nervous, would like to take the chance to get off to bed. No? You're quite sure? Well, don't complain afterwards that I didn't give you fair warning. This happened in India, in a little-known

81

province on the North-west frontier, in the year 1901 . . .'

The suggestively modulated voice rose and fell, the glow from the fire tinted the rapt surrounding faces of the boys, the coals shifted, and the wooden Cavern creaked with startling irregularity. Once Ian caught Blazer's eye and smiled his approval of the reconciliation with Denis. But he could not tell if the master noticed. The redness of the fire was reflected from his grizzled hair; tiny flames seemed to burn beneath his shadowy brows; occasionally a long white tooth glittered. The story that he told concerned an Indian youth who suffered a cataleptic stroke and was laid out for dead. At the point at which the relations of the youth were preparing him for the funeral pyre, and he stirred and spoke to them, Blazer screamed. His unexpected and horrific scream frightened the boys almost out of their wits. Some stood up, exclaiming, some seized others in the darkness. But then they began to laugh. The story, and The Singsong, ended. Blazer Whitlock's popularity, which had fluctuated throughout the term, rose to a new peak. Even Ian, gratified by it after all, and because he would soon be home and out of reach of the master, felt fonder of him than for ages.

By a Christmas post an envelope addressed in Blazer's thin complicated writing arrived for Ian. It contained a letter, a five pound note and a slip of paper. On the slip was written: 'Trayler, please keep the fiver to yourself, don't mention it to anyone, and don't think you've got to send me a present because I've sent you one. But you can write and thank me, remembering all the good manners you've been taught at Beaman's School!' Ian pocketed the banknote and burnt the slip of paper, then read the letter.

'My dear Trayler,' it ran, 'this is just to wish you a happy Christmas. Also the same to that brother of yours, if he remembers me. Don't eat too much and make yourself ill. Nothing exciting goes on here, but I'm devising some good torments for the Fifth Classical Form next term. Best wishes, B.W.'

Ian mentioned this letter to William, who was not interested. Early in the new year he answered it, thanking for the five pounds and for two more letters he had received. But one of these was endless, he had not read it at all, and so omitted to reply to some question of Blazer's, who wrote curtly: 'Dear Trayler, the least you can do is to read what I take the trouble to write to you. Sincerely, B.W.' In time, Ian answered this letter too.

Mr Hyde

O NCE A WEEK Ian spent an hour with Mr Hyde, who was preparing him for confirmation. In the master's bed-sitting-room they sat in wing chairs on either side of the fire, only lit in the coldest weather, while Mr Hyde discoursed incomprehensibly on subjects such as the Communion Service, Transubstantiation, the Laying-on of Hands and the Holy Trinity.

Ian was being confirmed for the simplest of reasons, because Mr Hyde had suggested it. He said his prayers, Our Father and Gentle Jesus, as he had been taught at home, but was not very religious, except in times of stress. On one occasion, in his first days at Beaman's School, he had failed to complete some Latin verses for Mr Beaman, had been kept in late, and, in his terror of being beaten, had fallen onto his knees in the empty classroom and prayed fervently to be delivered from evil. He had been surprised in this embarrassing position by Walter the bootboy, who was actually about ninety and always wore plimsolls, and had silently entered the room with a bucket of coal.

Yet Ian looked forward to being confirmed, because he likened it in his mind to at least a spiritual coming-of-age, because boys who went to the early service were excused evening chapel on Sundays, and because confirmation would mean no more of the padre's preparatory talks.

There was something uncanny about Mr Hyde. Blazer Whitlock called him 'Jekyll and Hyde'. He was extremely cruel in class; but in chapel, especially when he was blessing the boys – his deep-set grey eyes soulfully raised, a cassock and surplice of fine linen concealing his long body – he seemed to belong in a stained-glass window.

Ten days before Ian was confirmed, as their hour together was coming to an end, Mr Hyde rose to his feet and said: 'I was given a present yesterday. I wonder if you'd care to share it with me,' and crossing to a large clothes cupboard, he knelt suddenly on one knee, pulled out the heavy drawer at the bottom and produced a banana.

Ian thought it strange to keep a banana in a drawer, with clothes and things, but said he would like to share it very much.

Mr Hyde then produced a pocket fruit-knife with a mother-of-pearl handle and asked where he should cut the banana, what would be fair – 'Here? Or there? Here?'

Ian said, 'Yes,' and Mr Hyde divided the fruit, rotating it against his curved and flexible thumb.

The knife seemed to be as sharp as a razor.

Ian was handed his portion.

While he was attempting to peel it, a task he found surprisingly difficult, Mr Hyde remarked, peeling his own portion with easy flowing movements with the aid of the knife, and so affording fresh proof of his uncanniness: 'I want to ask you a question. I think we're good enough friends to talk quite freely.' He was always referring to this friendship. 'Do you understand what is meant by the Immaculate Conception?'

Although Ian had no idea what the words meant,

except that they referred to the process of birth, which was awesome and not to be discussed, at any rate with Mr Hyde, he blushed and said. 'Yes, I think I do, sir.'

'You know the facts of life, Ian?' asked Mr Hyde, dropping his banana peel into the waste-paper basket.

'Yes, sir.

'Shall I peel your banana for you?'

'No, sir, I can manage.'

'Can you? I don't think you can. Won't you have my half?' As Ian hesitated, Mr Hyde looked up, his eyes pale and probing. 'No one will have the advantage, we were completely fair, weren't we?'

'It wasn't that,' Ian said, smiling uncomfortably and exchanging bananas with Mr Hyde, who lowered his eyes without comment and resumed his expert peeling.

'You would be frank with me, wouldn't you, Ian?' he asked after a pause.

'Yes, sir,' Ian said, taking a large bite at his banana.

'You know how babies are born' – again he dropped the banana peel in the waste-paper basket – 'do you?'

'Oh yes, sir,' Ian mumbled, his mouth full.

'Have you known for long?'

'Oh yes, sir.'

'Who told you?'

Another slight pause.

'My brother, sir.'

'Are you sure, Ian? There's nothing you'd like me to explain?'

'Oh no, thanks, sir – I understand it all.'

'I see.'

Mr Hyde raised his banana, gazed at Ian unfathomably over the top, and nibbled it. Ian, feeling stunned by his lies, swallowed the remains of his bit of banana whole, said good night and hurried away.

He was to be confirmed on the Saturday of the following week. On the Thursday evening he went along to Mr Hyde's sitting-room for the last time, hoping to escape with one more relatively restful unintelligible discourse. But Mr Hyde began by asking if, before being confirmed, Ian would like to make his Confession. He said that although the practice of Confessing was not general in the English Church, he personally preferred to bring his boys to the Bishop in a pristine state. But Ian would have to think the matter over, he allowed, and therefore he would not return to it until a little later on.

Ian decided to decline the offer. Throughout their talk he racked his brains for a suitable excuse. Eventually Mr Hyde reverted to the subject by saying: '. . . After you've made your Confession, provided of course that you desire Absolution.' Ian was about to reply when the padre added: 'It may interest you to know that Denis' – Denis Preston, who was also being confirmed – 'wishes to make his Confession and hopes you will keep him company.'

'Oh well . . .' Ian said. 'Does he? Well, then, perhaps, yes . . . All right, sir.' But he felt furious with Denis.

Mr Hyde passed him a big white printed card. Ian glanced at it and read somewhere in the middle: 'I have been unclean, a, in deed, b, in word, c, in thought.' But in his alarm he misunderstood the sentence, so that it seemed to run: 'I have been unclean indeed . . .' Mr Hyde said he believed Ian would find the card of great assistance, and told him to mark with a tick the sins he had committed, and with a cross those he had not.

'Sir, may I write extra things on the card?'

Mr Hyde looked rather startled, but said yes, if necessary. He then instructed Ian to come to the chapel at six o'clock on the next day.

For twenty-four hours Ian studied and marked his card. He spoke of it to no one. Three times he wrote on it, 'I have smoked cigarettes,' and three times erased the words. Unfortunately his rubber was of the hard and gritty variety, it scarred the surface of the card, and a new fear possessed him, that not only God but also Mr Hyde would know of his deception. At five to six on the Friday evening he and Denis, sheepishly clutching their cards, met in the school yard and walked through Hall into the chapel.

Mr Hyde in cassock and surplice was standing by the altar. He suggested in a conversational tone that they should all pray for a moment. Ian prayed his concealment of the sin of smoking might not be detected, then was summoned by Mr Hyde, left his pew, and was directed to kneel on the blue carpet of the altar steps on one side of the altar rail, while the padre sat at a right angle on the other, in a wooden chair with the high back carved in the shape of a cross. His Confession began. He read out from the card the sins he had ticked, 'I have been proud, I have been greedy . . .' speaking in a tremulous undertone into Mr Hyde's ear. But he finished much too quickly. And there was a pause in which he thought: I must have sinned more than that, so few sins are bound to sound fishy.

Mr Hyde asked to see the card.

'Is this all?' he inquired, having perused it.

'Yes, sir,' Ian said, praying to God to support him in his lie.

'You know that whatever you tell me now is private and in confidence, don't you, Ian?'

'Yes, sir.'

'Have you nothing else to confess?'

'No, sir.'

'It's a grievous sin to lie when you're confessing, you know that?'

'Yes.'

'You have nothing on your conscience?'

'No.'

'No association of any sort?'

'What?'

'No associations with other people?'

'I've smoked,' Ian blurted out.

'Smoked?'

'I've smoked cigarettes.'

'Oh. Nothing else?'

'No. No, sir, nothing else.'

'I see.'

As he echoed the words with which he had concluded their talk the week before, Mr Hyde twisted his head, regarded Ian in the same enigmatic manner, and, telling him not to sin any more, absolved him.

Ian returned to his pew, exchanging a smile with white-faced Denis on the way. The mutter of lowered voices reached him. He felt infinitely relieved, and suddenly undistracted, pure and good.

The next day, Saturday, he was confirmed, and early on the Sunday morning he knelt on the blue carpet of the altar steps by Blazer Whitlock who had insisted on being present at his first Communion, and received from Mr Hyde, along with another uncanny smile, the consecrated Bread and the Wine.

Snapshots

Eternal Feminine

A BLACK CAT LAY on a windowsill in the sunlight, fast asleep.

The time was eleven o'clock on a summer's morning, the scene a quiet street in London. Children were playing cricket against a wall which jutted out at right angles from the line of houses. Every so often the ball was bowled past the right-angled wall, bounced along the pavement and finished in the gutter. A girl aged nine or ten fetched it. She chucked the soft ball back almost like a boy. She had a fair complexion, straight green-gold hair, and was wearing a pink shirt, a green pullover, green tartan trousers, white socks and sandals.

She was in the act of fetching the ball when she first noticed the cat asleep on the sill of the window of a ground floor front room.

She paused by railings across the basement area of the house in question and called gaily over the open space: 'Hullo, Pussy! Hullo, Puss!'

The cat did not move. It was lying in an abandoned attitude of total relaxation and contentment, with the tip of its fluffy black tail hanging down the wall.

The girl returned to join in the game. But now whenever she fetched the ball she stopped to talk to the unresponsive cat. Swinging on the railings she would say, 'Pretty Puss,' or make kissing noises with her pursed lips, or imitate the barking of a dog, or exclaim, 'Mice, Puss, mice!'

Once, lazily or irritably, the cat flicked its tail. And once it raised its head, opened its yellow eyes and squinted balefully into the sun. But on the whole it paid not the slightest attention.

In time the children, bored with their game of cricket, began to ride up and down the street on their bicycles, weaving between the parked cars. The girl in tartan trousers, who rode a shiny new bicycle a size too big for her, ignored the shouts and challenges of her playmates. Unsteadily she wheeled round in circles, pedalling along the pavement and bumping into the road; but she soon turned back to the railings, where she hopped to a halt and resumed her one-sided conversation across the basement area.

'Oh Pussy,' she said, 'please come here, Puss-cat. I want to stroke your fur and make a fuss of you. You're such a pretty puss. Won't you even come and say hullo? Please, Puss!'

She smiled at the cat, gazed at it and spoke in seductive accents, gently reproachful or sentimentally imperative. Her hair, brushed back from her forehead and fastened with a clip, gleamed gold in the sunlight. The loose hair round her ears framed her plump face, which was pink and white beneath a pale tan. She dismounted from her bicycle, crouched, extended her arm through the railings, clicked and twiddled her fingers enticingly, and repeated over and over again. 'Oh Puss-cat!' until the words became a sort of incantation.

At last the cat woke. It stared at her deeply, flicking its tail. Then it stretched a hind leg and yawned, showing a curly salmon-coloured tongue. For a few minutes it lay

94

in its luxurious position on the sill, slackly, on its side, listening to the blandishments of the girl. The slow blinking of its eyes, the quick flicking of its tail, seemed to denote indecision.

It sat up.

'Oh Puss!' she cried. 'What a pretty puss, what a beauty you are!'

As if to show its indifference, the cat started to lick a paw in an absorbed and business-like way. But then it stood, arched its back, hoisted its tail and rubbed itself against the sashes of the window, watching the girl and appearing to weigh her intentions. Abruptly it leapt from the sill onto the wall of the porch of the house, and dropped into the shadow at the top of the front steps.

The girl had hurried to the gate in the railings, which was in line with the steps and the garden path. But the cat was sitting down, eyeing her suspiciously. 'Oh Puss, sweet Puss!' It scratched its ear with movements like lightning. 'Oh Puss!' And it descended the steps and advanced along the path to meet her, mewing as if with confidence and affection.

At the same time one of the other children flashed past on his bicycle and called out: 'Hey, it's Jimmy, d'you see?' – pointing to a long-legged boy at the end of the street.

The girl hesitated, straightened up, looked at Jimmy, looked at the cat, which was twining itself round her ankles, and said to it: 'You funny little thing, what do you want? I haven't got time to play with you now.'

And she jumped on her bicycle and swung away.

Love Scene

A BLACK AND WHITE tomcat pushed his way through some long grass in the shadow of a cedar tree, carrying a mouse in his mouth.

The cat was broad-headed and had heavy hindquarters. He emerged into sunlight on a mown lawn, deposited the mouse, walked on, sat down and gazed absentmindedly into the middle distance.

It was summer. The garden air was sweetened by the scents of hay and roses. Bees sped like arrows across the garden in their search for nectar, while large flies circled and zoomed. Pigeons cooed and clapped their wings in the recesses of a wood not far away.

The mouse lay motionless. It was like a tiny greyish undulation of the surface of the lawn. Its lustreless fur was ruffled.

But the mouse was not dead. It crouched in an upright position, head lowered, no bigger than a man's thumb, with perfectly round black eyes.

And after a moment it began to move stealthily, a fraction of an inch at a time. It held itself so rigidly, and its feet were tucked so secretively under its body, that it resembled a toy mouse on wheels. It advanced, or rather retreated, towards the long grass, in which it might have taken refuge. Yet at the very edge of the lawn, almost where the longer grasses grew, it paused, stopped and turned. For unknown reasons, probably because fear or injury had robbed it of its sense of direction, it crept right back to within striking distance of the cat.

The latter had paid not the slightest attention to these manoeuvres. But now, tearing his gaze from whatever he found or had pretended to find interesting in the distance, he fastened curious yellow eyes on the mouse. Then he stood up, raised a black bulbous paw indecisively, flashed it out boxer-fashion, and sat down again, watching and waiting for his victim's reactions.

Whether or not the flashing paw actually touched the mouse, it served to shock and freeze the little creature into immobility.

The cat extended his front legs, sank down on the lawn, humping his back, and stared at the mouse with an uncertain brooding expression on his broad face. He too stayed still, except for the tip of his tail, which flicked electrically.

Time elapsed.

It was as if the cat was the first to give in. Impatiently he stood and raised a paw, but indecision got the better of him and he lowered it again. He seemed to be annoyed with himself for having checked the forgiving and friendly overtures of the mouse, also for not knowing what to do next, and in an abrupt movement at once irritable and flirtatious he rolled over, showing the white fur of his belly and kicking with kittenish abandon. He righted himself, lay for a moment in an attitude of sprawling relaxation, arose and began to nudge and tap the mouse with his paw. More often than not his tentative and even sympathetic gestures were arrested in mid-air.

The mouse responded to this encouragement by moving on its minute front feet and long thin silver-coloured back ones. But it must have been hurt, wounded, scratched by invisible claws. It hobbled uncomfortably, and straight at the cat.

He looked down at it with a sort of excited nervous tenderness. He gave it a provocative playful buffet. Another buffet knocked it on its side. He sniffed it and seemed sorry, and sat back on his heavy haunches in a disappointed and dejected manner.

But the gallant mouse struggled to its feet, and resumed the debilitated hobble towards the arbiter of its fate.

He celebrated by jumping on it. As if with relief, really as if with affection, he now stalked, sprang at and held the mouse between his paws. When his playmate remained for too long on its side or back, he would revive it after a fashion with quick-fire blows. The concentrated look in his unblinking yellow eyes showed that he was enjoying himself. In a final transport of feline pleasure he rolled over, tossed the mouse in the air, caught it on sharp curved claws and threw it like a ball from one paw to the other.

The mouse fell on the lawn and lay in a grey heap.

The cat sat up and licked a paw rather disgustedly. He nudged the lifeless mouse. He tapped it, seized it in his mouth, shook it and dropped it. At intervals he continued to worry and try to revive the corpse. Sitting beside it he looked disconsolate.

In due course he padded off to hunt in the long grass.

Femme Fatale

HER CHRISTIAN NAME was another heavy burden for her to bear through life: she was called Grace.

She was the opposite of graceful. She began by crawling clumsily and crushing her toys. In her teens she flopped about and was apt to fall over. Finally the epithet 'lumbering' applied to her: she seemed to have to heave her bulk into any form of mobility.

Throughout girlhood Grace Harningham was too big for her age. She developed great quivering buttocks and calves before puberty, and then a formidable bosom. Aged seventeen she was six feet tall and weighed eleven stone. At school she was called Queen Kong, Kong for short. Although she took her school-fellows' teasing, and everything else for that matter, in good part, she grew increasingly self-conscious and shy with strangers.

She looked at herself in mirrors with regret and reluctance. She had small eyes, a potato nose and a receding chin. Her complexion was pasty and her skin so greasy that powder, if she used it, clogged in the pores and caused spots. Her hair was thin and mousey, her teeth prone to decay.

Her obvious lack of sex appeal saddened her the more because she had a romantic tender disposition. She made the acquaintance of sadness early on, when she realised that her mother had died giving birth to her. As a young woman she ached for a man to love, and again in vain for a husband and children.

Towards the end of her schooling, her father asked what she wanted to do and become. Her prompt reply was: his secretary and assistant.

Reginald Harningham was a Conservative MP and a director of several companies. He was the son of a tailor in Northampton; had climbed the social ladder by means of scholarships, effectiveness, reliability and a certain charm; and had married late, happily and briefly. He was big and broad, the public figure type, boastful about his achievements, charitable, impersonal.

He believed he had brought up Grace, and that he loved her with all his heart and soul. But in fact he delegated her upbringing to Rose Marshall, her nursemaid who became his housekeeper. Rose, a kindly widow, already getting on in years when she took charge of the motherless babe, continued to provide Grace with the care and attention that he had no time for.

Reg Harningham was proud of being able to afford a house in his Northamptonshire constituency and a flat in Westminster; and he dragged Grace and Rose from one to the other and back again, although, wherever they were, days could pass without their even meeting. Nevertheless, and perhaps rightly, Grace clung to the idea that he was devoted to her; and she honoured and hero-worshipped him, not least because he took so little notice of people in general and herself in particular, and was so uncritical.

All the same her stated wish to be his secretary was a counsel of despair. It was a repudiation of, a flight from, the great cruel world that seemed to be peopled by prettier happier girls and the men who desired them only.

Grace Harningham's work for her father excluded social engagements. She steadfastly refused to accompany him to the lunches and dinners, the fund-raising dances and the functions, that he attended on most days and nights. She had no objections to meeting his political and commercial colleagues in office hours, and could forget to be shy with government ministers and powerful tycoons on business bent. But she dreaded the various humiliations bound to be meted out to her unattractiveness in society.

Reg Harningham, wrapped up in his own affairs, did not pry into her private life – he was not interested in it.

Once in a blue moon, after it was established between them that she preferred not to socialise in his company, he would ask: 'Have you got something amusing to do this evening, dear?'

And she would reply, 'Yes, Father,' and he would comment, 'Good, good!'

He also absent-mindedly repeated a familiar and regretful refrain, pitying Grace for having no known surviving relations on either her mother's or his own side.

Yet Grace was glad not to have busybody aunts and cousins trying to marry her off to reluctant suitors. What 'amused' her in her 'free' time was to stay at home with Rose Marshall, watching television in the evenings or walking for miles with her mongrel collie Ben.

She lavished affection on Ben, and took him for those walks in town or in the country, winter and summer. Occasionally in dark London parks and sequestered streets she was accosted by strange men, from whom she escaped, lumbering away, with a deep sense of the irony of her behaviour. Sometimes, as a result of such episodes or because she had observed one pair of lovers too many, she would shed tears of frustration.

She still hoped for love, the true sort, that a miracle would happen, that Prince Charming would materialise from nowhere, and his first kiss – and hers for that matter – would encourage her to dare to be free of her father and the apron strings attaching her to Rose; and having ceased to feel inferior and inadequate, she would at last be able to take her rightful place in the world and hold her head high.

Unfortunately, following the little dinner party for three to celebrate her twenty-first birthday, dear old Rose was taken ill, and her illness turned out to be cancer. She lived for five more years, thanks to Grace's nursing, and died at the respectable age of eighty-two.

At her funeral Grace cried and cried with a mixture of sorrow, relief and guilt: guilt because she was ashamed of her ungrateful feelings of liberation.

In the course of the next two years the restored brightness of her secret hopes dimmed and were almost extinguished. When her father suffered his disabling heart attack, she was at once very sorry and again contrarily relieved to have to set aside her personal aims and impossible ambitions for the foreseeable future.

Reg Harningham ailed and deteriorated for nearly a decade, throughout which he was enabled to pursue his career by his daughter's unremitting care and her resourcefulness. They were both characteristically stoical: they gave no outward sign of regretting the respective facts that his life and her youth were ebbing away. Their relationship, although physically closer, remained cheery and practical. He depended on her more and more, and now boasted privately and publicly that her admirable attitude to himself was not the least of his achievements.

He died suddenly, impersonally as it were, avoiding sentimental scenes, in the night.

Grace at thirty-six was a sadder and, because her father's small fortune had been latterly and largely spent on prolonging his existence, a poorer woman than – with better luck – she might have been. She resigned herself to her spinsterish fate; sold the leases of the Westminster flat and the Northamptonshire house; bought a cottage at the end of a cart-track near Market Astell in Suffolk; and retired there with her second collie dog called Ben and just enough money to live on.

At four-thirty in an afternoon of the next summer a saloon car turned off the main road and bumped along the cart-track to Forest Cottage.

Grace was warned of its approach by Ben's barking. She was in the patch of garden at the back, wearing a ragged old shirt that had belonged to her father and darned corduroy trousers. She lumbered indoors and peeped through her sitting-room window, but could neither see nor think who her visitor might be. Then, although aware of looking even more of a fright than usual, hospitality got the better of her and she stepped through the front door, smiling and telling Ben to shut up.

A chauffeur in uniform now ventured to leave the Daimler car, and, saluting her respectfully, opened one of the rear doors and began to help an ancient gentleman to get out.

Grace recognised him and spoke his name. He took no notice, would not look in her direction, rearranged his blue overcoat fussily and waited to be handed his walking-stick. At length he was ready, turned, smiled at her and spread his arms wide, as if to embrace her or be embraced.

She repeated her greeting and his name, Lord Duckwell, did the embracing, but cautiously, in case she knocked him over, and apologised for her appearance. He brushed aside so trifling a matter with a slight shrug of his bent shoulders and asked if she would be good enough to provide a cup of tea.

'Oh yes – please – do come in,' she said. 'What about your chauffeur?'

'Not necessary,' Lord Duckwell replied.

The chauffeur, who had overheard her question, reinforced his employer's negative. 'I have acquaintances to visit in Market Astell, Miss.'

Grace led the slow procession into the cottage.

Her guest had been her father's friend: they had served together on boards of directors. Alf Duckwell was another self-made man, a cockney builder who had become the boss of a huge civil engineering company, a knight and a life peer. Grace had met him quite often over the years: that is to say she had been introduced and re-introduced to him, then ignored. She again felt rather alarmed by his chilly self-possession, and wondered why on earth he had called on her.

She tried to usher him into the sitting-room, but he said: 'You won't be boiling your kettle in there. Show me where you usually have tea.'

She took him into her minute and untidy kitchen, removed his overcoat, sat him down at her shelf of a table, shyly put out crockery, cutlery and cake, made the tea and seated herself in the other hard wooden chair.

'How's Lady Duckwell?' she enquired.

'I lost her six months back,' he replied. 'Don't be sorry. You don't need to be sorry for not knowing. We had a good life together, and she wasn't ill for long.'

Grace exclaimed in tones of embarrassment and sympathy: 'Oh dear!' She had liked common warm-hearted Daisy Duckwell better than her husband.

Lord Duckwell changed the subject briskly, even brusquely: 'Tell me about yourself, my dear.'

She was so confused by this time, by his presence, and unheralded arrival, and her mistake and having no sandwiches, that she answered with inconsequential jerkiness: 'I'm fine. But I feel awful . . . Will you have a bit of this cake? I wish I'd known you were coming . . . You must be lonely.'

'That's why I'm here,' he said.

She queried, startled: 'Oh?'

'I've been thinking of loneliness, mine and probably yours,' he continued.

She could not look at him. She was afraid of what he might be going to say next. She caught a worrying glimpse of his wrinkled liver-spotted hand crumbling the cake on his plate. He was older than her father, a nearly bald, rather paunchy, rheumaticky octogenarian with white rings round the irises of his eyes and darkly discoloured eye-sockets.

He spoke again in his thick old precise dominant voice with its residual cockney inflections: 'And I'd like you to think something over, Grace.' He pronounced her name

Grice. 'You know me – I don't waste time – I'm here to give you something to think over. Would you like us to keep each other company? Will you see me through?'

She was blushing crimson and sweating and stuck in the same position with her head down.

'You can say the word and I'll stop.' He paused. 'Very well – since you haven't said it I'll go on – and maybe you'll have done yourself a favour in hearing me out. I saw you being a kind good girl to your father, and I heard him singing your praises. I trusted Reg's judgment, I still trust my own, and now I'm putting my trust in yours. Any rate – these are the pros and cons of my offer – apologies in advance for being blunt. First, the cons are that I'm eighty-two years of age, not too fit, no good for love, and used to getting my own way. The pros are that I could give you a position in the world and more than enough money, and I'd do my level best to be nice to you, and I won't last long. Shall I put my offer in a nutshell? Marry me! I believe and hope we'd do better together than we're doing separately and alone. There, I've shocked you; but I'll have to remind you nonetheless that I can't allow you much time to respond to my proposal. Show me where your lavatory is, and then, when I get back, we'll talk the matter over at least like friends.'

He stood up with some difficulty.

She jerked out in a broken tone of voice: 'Oh Lord Duckwell!' – not moving.

'Come come, dear,' he rallied her with dry humour, 'since when has a proposal of marriage made a girl unhappy? And considering what I've just been asking you, don't I deserve to be called by my Christian name?'

Grace laughed in a hiccupy tearful fashion, flashed half

106

a glance at her suitor with little red eyes in her big red face, and helped him upstairs to the bathroom.

By special licence, and deservedly in white, she married him in the church in Market Astell, and became Lady Duckwell. His best man was his friend and contemporary Lord Saxmundham, and she was given away by Alf's chauffeur, Bailey by name, who was not much older than she was.

Between becoming his fiancée and becoming his wife Grace had not seen Alf; but encouraging messages reached her via his secretary. All the arrangements were made by this lady, Mrs Williams, a kindly and approving sixty-year-old, who travelled up from London to Suffolk with a selection of engagement rings, met the parson, ordered the printed marriage service sheets, booked a suitable room and chose the food for the so-called wedding breakfast.

The bride-to-be was too bewildered and diffident to interfere. She let herself be guided by Mrs Williams, except in one particular: she would issue no invitations, she would ask no one, to the wedding – whence Bailey's unconventional role in the proceedings. Grace was shy both about her own appearance and the seniority of the bridegroom, and feared they would look a ridiculous couple.

Nevertheless, in spite of her readiness to bridge the generation gap, she was momentarily shocked by the spectacle of the two decrepit and overdressed gentlemen with walking sticks waiting for her at the altar.

But she made her vows sincerely: Mrs Williams had

advised the parson to cut the one referring to mutual bodily worship.

The congregation consisted of a few elderly ex-employees of Duckwell Engineering, Alf's lawyer, stockbroker and accountant, Mrs Williams, and the staff of his house in Smith Square, Westminster, his butler Evans, his cook May and his daily ladies, plus spouses. After the ceremony there were introductions and a buffet lunch at the White Hart in Market Astell, then the bride changed into one of her shapeless tweedy dresses and, sitting in the back seat of Alf's Daimler with Ben, while the bridegroom dozed and snored in the front passenger seat, she was driven to her new home by Bailey.

The Duckwell residence was the stranger for being so luxurious. It had thick carpets on the floor and a brightly cleaned and lit collection of Dutch pictures on the walls. Grace was the more confused by the contrast between her Cinderella-like situation and the debility of her Prince Charming. Alf had to struggle up the flights of stairs to show off her quarters, the former spare room and bathroom on the floor above his bedroom and dressing-room.

Between tea and dinner about a hundred persons not known to Grace arrived to drink the health of the newlyweds; and Harry Saxmundham stayed on to eat with the two of them. Alf's best man had been his best friend for many years, probably because he was the opposite or complementary type. Whereas Alf was of medium height, physically spare and mentally sharp, Harry was large in every sense, hulking and impulsive, with bushy eyebrows and a booming voice. Moreover he was an hereditary peer and had inherited the Crofton Castle estate in Warwickshire. What he had in common with Alf, apart from mutual affection, was widowerhood and childlessness.

His town house was just round the corner in Lord North Street.

At dinner Alf and Harry sat on either side of Grace and treated her with grandfatherly gallantry: they were both slightly tipsy. They paid her fulsome compliments, patted her, ended by toasting her in vintage port, and thoroughly embarrassed her, although she was flattered by and grateful for their attentiveness.

She was thankful when, at nine-thirty, Alf indicated that the party was over and kissed her good night: she had been afraid that he might get other uxurious ideas.

Later, in her bedroom above his, she was kept awake by a mixture of excitement and vain yearnings and regrets – and so heard the sinister thump and his subsequent moaning and groaning.

She put on a dressing-gown, plunged downstairs, listened at her husband's bedroom door and dared to enter. He was lying on the floor in considerable distress, having fallen and obviously broken some bone, and gazed at her with a fearful pleading expression on his ashen face.

'Oh Alf, don't die, please,' she cried, at which he seemed to be greatly reassured and tried to smile wan thanks in her direction.

She telephoned for an ambulance, roused the household, accompanied him to hospital, waiting while his hip was operated on and set, and from then on, for the remaining seven months of his life, scarcely left his bedside.

He never recovered his health: after his fall he had pneumonia, followed by heart attacks, little strokes, trouble with almost every part of his anatomy. Yet even as he was losing his life he would praise his wife for saving it.

'I wouldn't be here today,' he said repeatedly, while he was able to say anything, 'if she hadn't done the necessary.'

He told his friends, his doctors and nurses, and his staff that she was the kindest girl in the world, a welcome compliment from Grace's point of view, and at the same time a statement both self-congratulatory, since he had succeeded in marrying her, and indicative of his temporary suspicion that she might have let him lie and die on the floor of his bedroom.

That she was unmaterialistic, as he sometimes put it, in other words that she was not interested in his money, impressed him. In his gratitude and his pride, there was an element of surprise that she should genuinely wish to keep him alive. He tried to offer her access to his bank accounts, but she begged him not to bother his head with such trifles; he urged her to talk to his accountant, but she put off doing so. One day he reverted to his premarital promise to provide for her in the event of his death: she would be all right, he said. Then he added with touchingly untypical sentiment: 'But I don't want to think or talk of not being married to you.'

Harry Saxmundham introduced a lighter note into these discussions of the Duckwells' finances. He visited Alf constantly, and, on the rare occasions on which Grace happened not to be tending her husband, he would pretend to believe she had popped out to Cartier's. He teased her admiringly for spending nothing, and pitied her for being the wife of an unreconstructed miser.

Harry's jokes and blustery company were exceptional interludes in the history of Alf's fall and decline. The latter was amused less and less often, and able to assert himself in no more than two areas: he needed Grace, and he was romantic enough to stop her rendering intimate and disagreeable services. He and she spent almost all their married life in hospital, where competent nurses were on call. They would hold hands, or she would hold his shrunken bony hand in her large warm flabby one, for hour after hour without speaking.

Bailey drove her to and from the various hospitals involved, and waited for her patiently. And the people at Smith Square looked after her as best they could. And Alf's doctor, Dr Hardy, for the sake of her health banished her from the sickroom for four or five separate days of the seven long months of her vigil. Then she would motor down to Forest Cottage with Ben and Bailey, and air it, clean it, dig the garden, walk in the woods, and, sadness notwithstanding, enjoy herself and recover her composure.

Alf's end approached peacefully – his sleep deteriorated into coma. At last, one evening, she acknowledged the fact that he was slipping away from her, and when Harry turned up she could not help crying on his shoulder.

'What'll I do without him?' she sobbed and gulped explosively.

Whereupon Harry got redder in the face and more agitated, led her into an empty hospital rest room and addressed her thus: 'Grace, my dear, you mustn't worry about your future. No, really! Listen – forgive me for saying what I'm going to say, what I can't help saying, even though it probably shouldn't be said at this particular moment. But I've become so very fond of you, I must admit I've envied my old friend for having found you and married you. I can't imagine anything better than being taken care of by you, therefore I'd consider it the greatest possible honour if, circumstances permitting and in due course, you'd think of me as your suitor. Please do marry me one day, dearest girl – I couldn't bear to lose you after all we've been through together.'

Grace was dumbfounded. She almost fled from Harry. But she had another shock in store.

That same evening Dr Hardy, despite age and infirmity, arrived to take a probable last look at Alf, his patient for many years and his contemporary, and she again shed tears.

Having had her second cry on another male shoulder, she began to pull herself together, but then broke down completely.

Dr Hardy of all people, who seemed to her to have at least one foot in the grave, had said to her across the death-bed of her husband that he appreciated her caring attitude, he had quite fallen for her, and would like to see a lot more of her in days to come.

After Alf's funeral, Grace wanted to leave Smith Square and return to Forest Cottage.

But she remained in London for three reasons: to sign her name on a sort of conveyor belt of legal and financial papers; to comfort and not to desert Bailey and Mrs Williams and Alf's butler Evans, also May, his cook, who had become her friends and were now her dependants; and thirdly because of Harry Saxmundham, who, in a phrase as old-fashioned as he was, pressed his suit, pleading with her relentlessly to accept his proposal.

She had got over neither Alf's death nor her life with him. The suddenness of her marriage, and her second swift transformation from bride back into her customary role as the companion of terminal illness, had disconcerted her, despite her outwardly phlegmatic appearance. She was still trying to come to terms with aspects of her marriage, happy in a sad sort of way though it had been: for instance the age difference between Alf and herself, and its consequences; again, being the consort of a peer, called Milady and Her Ladyship, and in principle reigning over the little court of Alf's kingdom.

She required time and solitude, she longed for a lost normality, she half-wished to reclaim her maiden name. At the age of thirty-nine she was surer than she had been following her father's death that true romance would never come her way.

But what would happen to Bailey and Co. if she retired – retreated – into the shell of Forest Cottage?

And if she was going to be kind to Harry, not turn him down, not cast him off, she could not waste time – he was nearly eighty-three.

She mourned for two months, then married her second husband, again in white and with Bailey's assistance, in the chapel of Crofton Castle, becoming the Countess of Saxmundham.

Her abbreviated engagement to Harry had been a somewhat mixed bag. She was pleased that he was pleased, and grateful for his assistance with business matters: he told her, for instance, that she could easily continue to employ Alf's staff and maintain the house in Smith Square. That she seemed to be a very rich woman, and happened to be climbing the social ladder and about to queen it over a large estate, meant nothing positive to her: rather, she dreaded the new responsibilities and obligations. The potentially negative side of things was Harry's mounting ardour: she was afraid he might get a foolhardy urge to attempt to consummate their union.

In this pre-marital period Bailey drove her down to Crofton Castle to have lunch with her intended. The extensive park with deer, the great battlemented pile complete with moat and drawbridge, alarmed her; as, in another way, did Harry's apoplectic flirtatiousness. He showed her the eight-foot wide bed in the palatial room reserved for the wives of the Earls of Saxmundham, and his dressing-room in close proximity. Although she was too respectful of his age and position to tell him so, she tried to show by her demeanour and repressive actions that she could do without his bear-hugs and chucks under her receding chin, and was afraid of being the death of him. She did refuse to let him give her the diamond tiara which had been worn by his pretty first wife.

The unsettling question of age was raised with additional force at the wedding, since Harry's best man participated in a wheelchair. He was the nonagenarian Duke of Sussex, once a notorious womaniser and wag, but now a physical wreck, if a gallant one in his grey morning tailcoat with an orchid in the buttonhole.

The Duke again embarrassed Grace at the wedding breakfast. Sitting next to her, he interrupted the taciturn processes of mastication to say: 'I understand you've spent your life looking after old people. You're exactly the woman I want. I'll make a duchess of you, should Harry fall by the wayside. Remember, my dear!'

In the evening of that day a party with dancing was thrown for Harry's and indeed for Grace's employees and

114

tenants. The host and the hostess, who pleaded exhaustion, retired at about ten o'clock.

Upstairs Grace repeated that she was exhausted and that he must be, and gave him a hopeful kiss good night. He joined her nonetheless and without delay in the nuptial couch of the Saxmundhams and sought to exercise his matrimonial right, puffing and blowing, cursing and apologising. At length he removed himself into his four-foot half of the bed and instantly fell into stertorous slumbers. She lay awake, counting her mistakes and her blessings, wondering whether she was lucky or unlucky, and in time she too dropped off.

She woke to find her husband dead and cold.

Harry's funeral was celebrated in the chapel of his castle, or, precisely, of Grace's castle, five days after his and her wedding.

Immediately following the obsequies she was driven with her good dog Ben to Forest Cottage by Bailey, and she resisted the efforts of her lawyers and everyone else to persuade her to budge from there.

She had much business to attend to even while she recovered from the shock, or from shocks in the plural. She suggested that Bailey should take up residence in the White Hart in Market Astell and act as her intermediary with the outside world: an arrangement that proved satisfactory – he ferried visitors and documents to and from Forest Cottage.

Grace, Countess of Saxmundham, was now much more than very rich, since Harry too had left her everything. But she decided to renounce all her advantages that had accrued from the disadvantages – the deaths, bluntly – of her poor old husbands. She therefore instituted proceedings to give the Crofton Castle Estate to

115

Harry's remote Australian cousin, who had inherited the title, and to distribute Alf's fortune equally amongst the members of his staff. She was happier to have just enough money to live on, as before – her own money, she liked to think it was. She scrapped the idea of reverting to her maiden name: she honoured Harry and Alf, who had honoured her, by calling herself, at least conversationally, Grace Saxmundham.

After a few weeks of widowhood she received a note on coronetted writing paper in a shaky scrawl. The Duke of Sussex wrote: 'Now don't be a silly girl. Come here and we'll take care of each other.' Perhaps it was all for the best that the Duke expired at the end of the fortnight during which she had pondered the problem of how to reject her last suitor without hurting his feelings.

She determined not to marry again, and gradually she re-established the routine of her spinsterhood. But Forest Cottage was different, existence there was pleasanter by far, because no longer lonely. Every day, or almost, the Daimler bumped along the cart track and Bailey spent more or less time with his mistress. He did the heavy work and the shopping and the telephoning. He was Grace's secretary and her friend of proven reliability.

Bailey was forty-five years old, a tall man of heavy build, with black hair going grey, a handsome kind countenance, a cheerful loud laugh and a polite sympathetic manner. He had worked for Alf Duckwell for twenty-odd years, and had extended his loyal devotion to his boss's wife. He was unmarried and did not publicise his private life; but once, when he had been unusually subdued and Grace had asked him why, he replied: 'Just woman trouble, Milady.'

Although he had accommodation in London with

parking space for the Daimler, he said he was content to be living in Market Astell. He donned country clothes and took a lively interest in Grace's garden. She would cook a larger hot meal at midday, which they shared in her tiny kitchen. They went through paperwork, discussed practicalities, and reminisced about the late Lords Duckwell and Saxmundham, to whom he had given her in marriage. Their relationship remained formal – she still paid him wages; but she was not shy in his company, except insofar as she jibbed at asking him, and thought he might not like to be asked, to call her by her Christian name.

One afternoon, about a year after Harry Saxmundham's demise, Bailey had an accident. He was chopping wood at Forest Cottage, stepped backwards into an unseen rabbit hole and sprained his ankle, and let the axe fall and cut into his leg. He crawled indoors, he could not walk, and showed his bloody wound to Grace, who pushed him while he pulled himself upstairs and into her bedroom, made him lie on her bed and applied remedies and bandages to the best of her ability. He apologised for causing trouble and promised to be better shortly.

She hurried down to the kitchen to brew tea. She should have felt comfortable in the familiar situation of having an invalid on her hands. But she had realised, when she saw Bailey stricken, that he meant more to her in at least one respect than had Rose Marshall, her father, Alf and Harry: whereas they had depended on her, she depended on him.

She lumbered back to the bedroom, where Bailey said, after sipping the sweet tea and thanking her repeatedly: 'This will never do, will it, Milady?'

She returned: 'It's all right, don't worry.'

'Not just your waiting on me.'

'What?'

'I've been happy here in Suffolk, and nobody could have been kinder than yourself.' He hesitated and seemed to change the subject. 'I'll be able to drive to Market Astell in a little while. And maybe I ought to get home to London.'

'Oh no!'

'My wishes would be otherwise. I wouldn't want to give up my job and everything.'

'Oh no – what would I do without you?'

'I could say the same.'

She sat down abruptly on the creaking wicker chair in the bedroom, blushing and trembling, not looking at him.

He continued: 'I've a great admiration for you. I've never got on this well with anyone else. Forgive the impertinence – but it's impertinence or nothing. I'd marry you if I could. I've got the money to support you, since you've been so generous with His Lordship's funds.'

After a tense pause, without moving, not daring to move, in a low thick voice she spoke the words that conceded everything: 'Oh Bailey!'

A week or so later they had broken through enough nominal, social and emotional barriers to be able to reconsider the question of matrimony.

Grace Saxmundham objected half-heartedly to Tom Bailey's proposal thus: 'I seem to have a fatal effect on husbands. If you were my husband I'd be even more worried about you and the state of your health than I am already.'

He replied: 'Isn't it third time lucky?'

The Happy Warrior

I NEVER KNEW THE cause of the fight, I was not involved in it, thank God.

The scene was the bar-room of my local, The Drum and Monkey, and the time of day about 1.30 p.m. I was sitting at a marble-topped table by myself at one end of the long low-ceilinged dimly glittering room, having a bite to eat, while, at the other end, a group of five or six men stood by the bar, drinking beer and talking and laughing somewhat rowdily. Several more men, apparently belonging to the same group, sat drinking at tables piled with dirty plates and cutlery.

I thought at first they were office workers out on a celebratory spree. But the group was exclusively male, and its members looked too husky and fit for work in an office. I concluded that they belonged to a sports association, probably a rugger club. But I could not imagine why they were all in a pub in the middle of a workday, nor was I particularly interested.

The space between me and them – the bar with bar-stools, gangway, and tables ranged along the wall – was peopled with the customary crowd, a kissing couple, pairs of girls together, busy businessmen, pensioners; and a jukebox was playing background music.

A voice raised in anger seemed to start it. There was the sound of scuffling, then a glass broke, a woman

119

screamed or squealed, and a short grey-haired man behind the bar who must have been the landlord was shouting, 'None of that, please! Steady, please – we don't want police in here!' And those unconnected with the combatants, hastily collecting coats and bags and brief-cases, retreated in the direction of myself and the exit doors behind me. Quite a few quit the place; the rest gathered round in such a way that I as well as they had a good clear view down the length of the room.

The landlord's pleas had been disregarded. He was now bellowing at the top of his voice: 'Cool it! Cool it, will you?' He got beer chucked at him for his pains, and then more glass was broken and ground underfoot. The seated men had joined the standing ones, for unknown reasons they were all furious, red to purple in the face, swearing hoarsely, and milling, shoving, pushing, slap-ping and trying to hit each other.

I had witnessed such fights before, on playing fields, at parties. Their common denominators, in my experi-ence, were the suddenness with which they broke out, and the almost pathetic untidiness of the actual fighting. The crisp exchanges of blows of actors in films, and boxer-type knockout punches, were again conspicuous by their absence in the bar-room of the Drum and Monkey. The fisticuffs reminded me of pat-a-cake, and the general activity of rugger scrums or so-called loose mauls.

On the other hand the explosive violence, both physical and emotional, was exciting and alarming. My heart thumped. I wondered if I ought to beat a retreat while I still could. There was a discordant symphony of noises: music and roaring, thumps and groans, shrieks from my female fellow-spectators and laughter and brave words of advice from a sporting male contingent, 'Sock him, kick him! Go for his eyes!'

Time passed, maybe only a minute or two: but there is nothing like a fight to make minutes feel like hours and thus to lengthen life, provided you survive to live it.

Apart from the bellows of the landlord, and the objections – I believe – of barmaids skulking somewhere out of sight, no serious effort to stop the fighting was noticeable. The roughhouse seemed to be getting rougher, if anything: somebody crashed to the ground and furniture splintered.

But now a taller beefier figure strode into the middle of the fray. He was thirtyish, ruggedly handsome and smiling. I thought he was going to call a halt to the bellicose proceedings. Instead he struck one man straight in the face with his huge fist, and another, again in the face or on the nose, with a vicious jab of his elbow; and I was sure I could hear bones breaking. Both victims were rocked backwards with blood literally spurting from their noses and mouths, and doubled up and disappeared from view. Their still smiling attacker was forcibly restrained by the many hands of his friends or his foes, and, amidst a chorus of shocked disapproval, either dragged back to the chair he had been sitting on or pushed through the pub's side door which was at that end of the bar-room.

The fight was over. The fighters who were visible mopped their brows and straightened hair and ties. Others knelt on the floor beside their two badly injured and prostrate companions. A barmaid carrying a bowl of water hurried towards these groups, and the landlord was obeying someone's instruction to dial 999 for an ambulance. A few spectators ventured forwards to gawp at the wounded, and people began to order drinks again, brandy in particular.

I left the Drum and Monkey, and ever since have as it were re-run the scene of trouble in my mind's eye, and pondered it.

What remains with me vividly is not the ultimate blows or the blood, but the smile of the man who dealt the former and shed the latter. At first it looked good-humoured, philanthropic: the lips were parted without tension, the teeth were faultlessly white: and he was surely not angry, he was neither hot nor bothered – and I expected him to differ still further from the other fighters by speaking up for peace and goodwill. However, in the split second before he lashed out I realised he was too cool to be true, the coolest of customers, and smiling because he was in his element and enjoying himself. And perhaps as his fist smashed face number one I saw, I got the idea, that his unchanging smile was bullying, ruthless, malicious and terrifying.

It was his power to hurt, and its exercise, that tickled his fancy; while humour, and humane feelings, were excluded from his hard glinting apology for a real smile. Although I had read about his type, I had never before come across anybody like him, nor have I since. He was the embodiment of that dreadful figment of my imagination, the giant who chases one, breaks into one's home, tortures one to death or almost, and laughs at one's pain. He was the merciless destroyer of the illusion that one is safe, or can get out of harm's way.

Yet no doubt in wars that type becomes a hero. After all my smiling pugilist in the pub was the image of the happy warrior.

Besides, more confusingly, it has to be remembered

that he and his strong-arm tactics finished the fight. In my experience and in the end he merited membership of the select company of peacemakers, who are blessed.

The Story of the Theme

IN THE BEGINNING was the word, declares St John in the first sentence of his Gospel. Very soon after the word, say I, was the story. Then along came the theme.

St John also declares in his first sentence that the word was God. The single syllable, God, is by now fraught with so many associations, questions and answers that it almost seems to be a story in itself. But in fact nouns are nothing much without verbs; nouns need verbs – like eggs they are fertilised by verbs. Omniscient God in His wisdom and mercy therefore did the necessary from a linguistic point of view: He at once created the verb and presided over the birth of story.

Let us humbly hope that the Almighty thought it good to be able to say, 'God is, God rules,' and in due course, 'I shall create heaven and earth'; and to have given His children the capability to describe life, also eventually to add thematic point and force to their stories of living.

Permit me to try to tell the difference between a story and a theme.

In short, a story is a record of events; a theme is the subject, argument or burden of a story.

Stories are either directly or by implication about people, creatures, live organisms, and the activity of existence. Every move we make, everything we think and feel, every spin of the earth is or can become a story, and every story refers to the eventful business of existing. The above is true even of our abstruse preoccupations: for religion is the story of God in the image of man, and of our faith in Him: philosophy is the story of how we do and how we should behave; astronomy is the story with which we attempt to plumb the mystery of the universe; science is the story of our curiosity.

When two or more words are strung together in a meaningful manner, the story, story-telling, art, logic and civilisation in all their potential glory are on the way: whence the progress, in the literary context, from *a cat sat*, to *the cat lapped milk*, to *the cat will eat/would eat/has eaten the bird*, and so on to *Hamlet* and *David Copperfield*.

Grammar has reason to believe that it is the mother and father, or at least the godparents, of the story. Grammar does lord it over meaning and sense, if rather presumptuously. On the other hand Shakespeare, without reference to grammar, linked together three extraordinarily evocative words, 'Night and silence' – which tell the story of a person or persons listening in the dark.

Here is another difference between stories and themes: the former are without number, uncountable, whereas I am about to suggest that the latter are capable of numerical limitation.

Definitions of the concept of the theme take a paradoxical turn. For instance: although a theme is not a story, every story has a theme. Again: themes and stories are separate and distinct things, yet indivisible. The theme is an important, even the most important, element of the story; but without its illustrative story it can look like any unimportant single word.

You ask me to come down to earth and explain.

125

Very well, and to put first things first, this is my personal list of themes. Yes, surprisingly no doubt, I would claim there are no more than seven themes of stories in the whole wide world:

1. LOVE
2. CONFLICT
3. RESURRECTION
4. RECOGNITION
5. EXPLORATION
6. FAITH
7. GENEROSITY

Obviously each theme by itself covers a wide range of experience; and each can be inverted, thus multiplying my seven by two. Each can also be combined with one or more others, creating extra omnibus themes.

LOVE, for instance, straightforwardly speaking is the theme of stories of sexual, platonic, maternal, paternal and filial love, of God's love and love of God, of spiritual and materialistic love, of love of the past, present or future, of love of self, and so on. CONFLICT is the theme of war, struggle on a physical, emotional, psychological or ideological level, of competition, ambition and victory. RESURRECTION is the theme of the New Testament, of Jesus Christ and the founders of other religions, of Lazarus, of Cinderella, of everyone who has suffered a circumstantial change for the better, or been rescued or redeemed. RECOGNITION is the theme of discovery, self-awareness, religious conversion, and the successful search for knowledge and truth. EXPLORATION is the theme of life itself; while the themes of FAITH and GENEROSITY require no explanation.

126

Again, LOVE, inverted, turned inside out, becomes the theme of hate; CONFLICT, of peace, tranquillity, passivity and defeat; RESURRECTION, of earth-bound pessimism and despair, of the story of moral as well as materialistic riches to rags; RECOGNITION, of the failure to discover, learn or find anything; EXPLORATION, of reactionary, stick-in-the-mud, timid and life-denying attitudes; FAITH, of doubt, disloyalty, distrust; and GENEROSITY, of jealousy, envy, greed, avarice and all sorts of meanness.

Thematically, I would analyse my mini-stories about that cat as follows. The story *a cat sits* illustrates the EXPLORATION/RECOGNITION/FAITH themes: the cat is exploring the possibility of sitting, recognising the fact that it is seated, and has had to have a touch of faith to attempt to sit. *The cat* which *lapped milk* is exploring, recognising, loving the milk, and may well be resurrecting itself by lapping it. *The cat will eat* largely illustrates the theme of FAITH; *the cat would eat* brings in the theme of CONFLICT, since the cat may be prepared to fight in order to satisfy its hunger; and *the cat has eaten the bird* puts CONFLICT ahead of various other themes, owing to the probability of there having had to be mortal combat before the meal.

As for *Hamlet*, every theme plus inversions figure in its story. Hamlet *loves* his dead father, has love–hate relationships with his mother and Ophelia, and hates the king, his stepfather. There is *conflict* throughout the play, but peace at the end, when all the chief players in the drama have been killed. Hamlet's father is *resurrected* in ghostly form; heaven is taken into consideration by everyone; but the Hamlet we see and know is consigned to the hell of despair. He *recognises* dirty work on the part of his mother and stepfather, and *explores* – investigates – the crime of their murder of his father; he *recognises* the necessity of just revenge, he *explores* the means of exacting it; but he misses the point of Ophelia's love for himself, and fails to look into the possibility that he will be poisoned to death. He has *faith* in his father rightly, and wrongly none in Ophelia. He *generously* risks and then gives his life to punish his father's murderers, but is jealous, suspicious, grudging and cruel in his ill-treatment of the girl who loves him.

The main theme of *Hamlet* is CONFLICT in the particular sense of revenge. CONFLICT is also the main theme of *Macbeth*, but in the sense of ambition. RECOGNITION, in view of the hero's changing relationships with his daughters, is the main theme of *King Lear*; and RESURRECTION in its mundane form is that of *Timon of Athens*, since Timon's story is like Cinderella's, except inverted – he falls just as she rises in the world.

Of *David Copperfield*, the main or the first of its many interwoven themes is LOVE.

The stories of Shakespeare and Dickens are extremely complex; but are stories ever simple?

A cat sits is an example of the possible shortness of a story; simplicity is another matter.

Stories so simple as to have only one of my seven themes would have to be reduced to the point of absurdity: I love you – LOVE; let battle commence – CONFLICT; life after death – RESURRECTION; eureka – RECOGNITION; where is he, she or it? – EXPLORATION; I believe – FAITH; all I have is yours – GENEROSITY.

And a second glance at such stories shows that neither in real life nor thematically are they as simple as they look. Amorous journeys rarely begin with one person saying to another, 'I love you,' nor do they end with lovers meeting: true romances which include those three little words combine the themes of EXPLORATION, RECOGNITION, FAITH and GENEROSITY with LOVE. The same applies to the other abbreviated stories or parts of stories above: the theme of each, expanded realistically, would be a combination of the positive and negative aspects of some or all my seven themes.

Gentle readers may object to my claiming to have whittled down the number of the themes of stories to seven, then to my attributing any number of subsidiary themes to each of the seven, and coolly suggesting that they can be used together to produce goodness knows how many.

My thematic story in answer is that, having EXPLORED the subject, I RECOGNISED certain salient features, and have FAITH in my research and deductions; but with my peaceable disposition am loath to enter into any sort of CONFLICT, would GENEROUSLY apologise for having misled my readers, hope we can therefore LOVE one another again, and promise I shall bury and not RESURRECT my theory if theirs is superior to it.

Creed for Yesterday?

I BELIEVE IN THE possibility of freedom from poverty, injustice and oppression.

I believe in equality of opportunity, in that equality which has long been preached and promised by our revolutionary masters and superiors.

I believe in the eventual glorious victory of the working class over the educated, cultured, traditional forces of reaction, which, according to the revolutionary interpretation of history, will surrender without fighting and are anyway doomed.

I believe in Marx, Lenin and Stalin, in communism and its saints and martyrs, and that all religions, together with their priests, idols and temples, should be destroyed.

I believe in a rule of law, or at any rate in the creation of a new just legalistic process, which will punish kings and queens and their children and the bourgeoisie, and protect and reward the poor masses.

I believe in art and the uncensored dissemination of information, so long as they serve the cause of the people. I believe in Trade Unions so long as they promote the interests of the people. I believe that the revolution will choose a leader who knows what is best for the people.

I believe my present duty is to take part in the class struggle, and protest, agitate, demonstrate, resist, strike against and generally disrupt decadent capitalist society.

When the battle is won, I shall be ready to shoot revision-ists and wreckers.

I believe that the revolutionary contract will be sealed irreversibly by blood and the shedding of blood. For this reason amongst others, lackeys of capitalism who have exploited the workers for centuries, the rich, bosses, the clergy, judges and lawyers, personnel of the armed services, and the political opposition, and independent-minded fathers of families, farmers, shopkeepers, householders and the self-employed, also ethnic minorities which might cause trouble, and idlers, gipsies and beggars, will have to be purged from our future social system.

Furthermore I believe a true people's army of secret police and loyal spies and informers will have to safeguard the ideological purity of the revolution and root out its enemies.

I believe in the rehabilitation of anti-social elements in labour camps, and that incurable objectors and dissidents should be regarded as insane and confined and treated in psychiatric hospitals.

I believe people should be persuaded by every available means not to look for help or mercy from any quarter except the revolution, represented by essential authority, namely the temporary dictatorship of the proletariat which is unlikely to last for more than seventy years.

I believe a revolutionary society needs to be distracted from its grievances, and therefore propaganda must counter hunger and hardship by whipping up fears of internal conspiracy and invasion by foreign powers.

I believe war is preferable to the admission that the revolution is failing.

It is an article of my faith that the masses will be happier to sacrifice even their lives for the revolution than they are in the meanwhile, competing with one another for material advantages and luxuries and selfishly enjoying themselves.

I believe we can and will create heaven on earth.

Modern Instances

Then and Now

Henry picked up Jake in his new secondhand open Morris Minor, and together they picked up Carol and her friend Jennifer and drove on to the dance.

Henry and Jake were seventeen and best friends at school. Henry was short, and the brown curly hair on his forehead made him look like a young bull. Jake was taller, fairer and willowy. Carol was a dim respectable blonde, also seventeen, with whom Henry thought he was in love. Jennifer turned out to be a year older, and with her prettiness and her poise she seemed much more adult. She had a lovely shiny elastic sort of skin and wavy chestnut-coloured hair.

It was long ago; winter; and even with the hood down the interior of the car was draughty. They all sat in their overcoats, Carol next to Henry in front, and Jake and Jennifer in the back seat.

Each of the boys paid for two tickets in the dance-hall, which was cavernous and brightly lit. The girls emerged from their cloakroom in knee-length silk dresses, and they began to dance, Carol with Henry, Jennifer with Jake.

The time was about nine o'clock, and they danced more or less nonstop until midnight. By arrangement, they had eaten before they met. When they were hungry again and thirsty, they bought sandwiches and soft drinks at a refreshments counter and sat briefly at a table for four, chatting and giggling.

Jake danced twice with Carol, otherwise with Jennifer.

He knew he danced badly with Carol, and guessed that he danced worse because she would apologise when he stepped on her toes. Holding her almost at arm's length, he could not stop her bouncing unpredictably. He liked her quite, but found her completely asexual. Whatever Henry had seen in her for the last six months was a mystery.

Both the boys were virgins. They were only just seventeen, and they were living in an era more romantic than permissive. They thought of girls day and night, especially at night: that is to say Henry thought of Carol, and Jake, who was susceptible or fickle, of one girl after another. But each could number the proper kisses he had had on the fingers of one hand. Henry had not yet managed to kiss Carol as he pined to.

Jake was pleased to discover immediately that he danced better with Jennifer. They moved in rhythmical unison, and when he went wrong she would look at him and correct him with provocatively smiling authority: 'No, no – it's like this – try again – d'you see now?' The fact that she was so old, eighteen years of age, added to her glamour. Besides, she was such fun – relaxed, yet lively and responsive: if there was something to laugh at, Henry making another of his laboured puns, a couple dancing strangely, she would catch Jake's eye or let him catch hers. She and Carol were doing a Domestic Science Course together. 'We're a couple of cooks,' she laughed.

As the evening progressed, Jake worried less about keeping in time to the music. Of course, he had rather fallen in love with Jennifer at first sight. Now he became aware of the lithe muscles on either side of her backbone under his right hand, and that an errant strand of her hair was tickling his chin. But his youth and inexperience largely transmuted these sensual delights into sentiment: his soul thrilled to the poetry of their relationship and censored low lustful considerations.

The band played swoony tunes before the Gallop and the National Anthem. He was startled and even more excited when Jennifer's temple made contact with his cheek. He was, they were at her instigation, dancing cheek-to-cheek, like lovers in films.

The final roll of drums and clash of cymbals were disappointing. Jake wished he could go on dancing with Jennifer for ever. They were joined by Henry and Carol, whose jokes and banalities jarred upon his mood.

Having collected their coats they trooped out of doors into the refreshing chill of early morning and seated themselves in the Morris Minor as before.

Jake had not dared to look at Jennifer since those last dances. He felt too shy, and fearful of all the possible mutual disappointments of close inspection.

But when they had driven out of town and into the country a fox loped across the road in front of the car, and he turned spontaneously to draw her attention to it. Their eyes met for a timeless moment, and hers twinkled as if with interrogative reassurance.

He had to decide what to do next. Could he, should he, kiss her? It was unthinkable in front of, or even behind the backs of, Henry and Carol. Anyway he doubted that she would permit such a liberty, and he lacked the courage simply to take it.

Henry now decreed that he would drop his friend at

home first: the implications being that he wanted to enjoy Carol's company for as long as possible, and that the car was bumping and rattling towards Jake's imminent good night and goodbye to Jennifer.

At the top of the hill exactly one mile from the parting of their ways, as it were, Jake slid his hand into the space on the seat between them. In the dark the others would be unlikely to notice it there. Besides, it was half-hidden by overcoats. He waited tensely, staring straight ahead. The small hand slipped into his was wonderfully warm and caressing. His heart pounded and he had to try to control his breathing.

The Morris Minor squeaked to a stop.

Jake thanked everybody, said it had been a grand evening, got out and stood on the pavement. At last he gazed yearningly at Jennifer, who smiled back at him through the grubby windows of the car and blew him a kiss while Henry drove on.

He loved her more than he had ever loved anyone before. Whether or not he would see her again did not worry or indeed occur to him. He could hardly be more excited and elated, and he felt fulfilled.

A quarter of a century later Jake was forty-two years of age; a stockbroker by profession, partner in a London stockbroking firm; the father of two teenage children and the ex-husband of Sally, who had remarried after their divorce on the grounds of the irreversible breakdown of the marriage; and the long-term lover of an adulterous wife, Martha, who could not or would not get rid of her impossible and proprietorial spouse.

Jake lived in a small flat in Chelsea. He was well off but had unluxurious tastes. He did not see enough of Martha, and was often lonely, in spite of working late, having a wide circle of acquaintanceship, and belonging to various clubs. He had lost touch with his schoolfriend Henry ages ago, and quite forgotten Jennifer.

One evening he dined with his colleague Michael and Michael's wife Sue and a friend of theirs, Anne, in a fashionable restaurant where a band played and patrons could dance.

He had hesitated before accepting Michael's invitation. As a rule he steered clear of merely social junketings. Moreover Michael and Sue were incorrigible match-makers, and had tried repeatedly to introduce him to Anne, who was also divorced, and reputed to be pretty and at a loose emotional end. He was committed to Martha, had been more or less faithful to her for years, and did not want to complicate the issue by getting involved with someone else: it was too late, he was too old.

On the other hand Martha had been absent for three weeks, holidaying with her husband on Pacific islands, and was not due back for another three. Since her attitude to Jake's love was irresponsible, why should he behave responsibly? It had happened before: what was he expected to do with himself in these loveless periods? Although she assured him that her marriage was a mere formality, she still sought to please her husband at her lover's expense, and so was entitled to no more of the latter's loyalty than he could borrow of hers.

Such grudging arguments were stale, he had had recourse to them on previous occasions, and they exacerbated his feelings of boredom.

139

It was in a bored and mildly curious spirit that he eventually fell in with Michael and Sue's plan.

He met the other three in the cocktail bar of the restaurant.

Anne was foreign – Austrian – by birth. She was in her late thirties, strongly if not solidly built, not really pretty but smart, a smart woman in every sense, and vital and uninhibited. In spite of having lived in England since she was a child, she spoke English with a rather exaggerated accent: it was meant to be funny and flirtatious. She had short brown hair and wore large golden earrings.

The four of them had a few drinks, then a lot to eat and more to drink. At ten o'clock or so Michael and Sue said they had to go home to relieve their babysitter, and begged Jake and Anne to stay on for as long as they wished. Michael added that he had paid for an extra bottle of wine in case his guests decided – in his suggestive phraseology – to make a night of it.

When Anne declared that she had no children, thank heaven, meaning she had neither reason nor inclination to leave the restaurant yet, Jake rose to the challenge of her bold glance and asked her to keep him company for a little longer and share Michael's wine.

He was instantly sorry he had done so. He was more than ever afraid that he would not be able to resist Anne's direct and earthy appeal. Alcohol had already introduced an element of recklessness into his conduct as well as obviously into hers.

They said goodbye to Michael and Sue and sat side by side in semi-darkness on the sofa-seat while the band played.

She broached the subject of his divorce: 'We're on our own and you're on your own, like me, aren't you?'

He agreed gloomily, and she rallied him thus: 'Aren't we lucky?'

And she continued with middle-European verve: 'I need to be free. I don't want to cook dinner for a husband, I want to laugh and dance. Please, come and dance with me now.'

On the tiny expanse of dance-floor she clamped her whole body against his: cheek-to-cheek was the least of it. They swayed speechlessly in the midst of other swaying couples for about a quarter of an hour.

Then she leaned back and looked at him with a knowing and quizzical expression, and murmured: 'Maybe it's time to go.'

In his car, which had been parked nearby, she told him where she lived and gave him directions. He missed one turning absent-mindedly, because he was wondering how best to say that he had decided to have nothing more to do with her. His ardour was cooled by her unmistakable availability: he was put off by her assumptions and impatience. He remembered Martha and suddenly yearned for her high-class fastidiousness and elusiveness.

He warned Anne without any preamble: 'I'm not as free as you may think.'

Her reply: 'Sorry,' was either a question, because she had not heard or understood him, or an expression of sympathy on account of his lack of freedom.

'I'm waiting to marry again,' he explained.

'Aren't we all, darling?' she commented satirically.

He regretted this exchange. He felt he had made a fool of himself, been clumsy and rude, appeared puritanical and unsophisticated. He was keen to repair the damage he had done. After all, he owed Martha nothing, except perhaps an act of revenge. He drove in argumentative silence, obeying Anne's instructions, until he pulled up outside the block of flats where she lived.

Gazing ahead through the windscreen, she put her hand on his thigh and remarked, as if throwing a further contribution into their intermittent discussion: 'But one must always try to be happy, and not waste time or worry, that's my philosophy.'

His agreement was reinforced both by penitence and by the position of her hand.

She turned to him and said in a tense and urgent tone of voice: 'Come in with me.'

He realised it would end with them making every sort of love known to experience. She was a stranger – he neither liked her very much nor trusted her, and he dreaded the trouble she was undoubtedly capable of causing if he gave her the chance.

'Yes,' he said, and followed her indoors with a heavy heart.

A Reason for Living

ARTHUR PENDLE IN his delirium repeated one word over and over again.

The word was 'waste'.

The various causes of his illness were flu, a heart attack, pneumonia, and, no doubt, the fact that his wife Margaret aged sixty-one had died three months previously.

Arthur Pendle himself was sixty-two. He had taken early retirement at sixty and left his job at the bank; Margaret had given up her work as receptionist at a dental practice; they had sold their house in East Croydon and bought a flat in Kemptown in Brighton. Their new home was lovely. They had a bedroom apiece, a south-facing sitting-room with views of the sea and a glassed-in balcony. They seemed to have everything to live for.

No wonder he muttered 'Waste, waste' on his bed of sickness and sorrow.

Arthur was a smallish neat quiet man, conscientious, more effective than he appeared to be, stoical and cautiously sanguine. He had gone into the bank straight from school, and was still living with his parents when, in his twenty-fifth year, he met Margaret at an East Croydon charity dance. She was a vivacious brunette, attractive, in demand and rather high-handed, who called him Mickey Mouse and refused to take his mild yet persistent courtship seriously. After three years of it he proposed to her or tried to: she interrupted him thus, 'Don't! Please! I'm not listening, I won't listen!'

But they continued to meet intermittently; and then she had to go abroad with her mother, who was apparently ill, for three months. On her return she was changed, gentler, humbler, and she accepted his second proposal with gratitude, tears and apologies.

Their marriage was like the curate's egg: good in parts, that is to say in the parts which were less intimate. Sexually, although she was not a virgin and he was willing and able, a certain lack of enthusiasm on her side inhibited him. The next disappointing thing was that due to some internal complication she could not bear children. Soon there was nothing romantic between them. On the other hand they were good friends: their relations were too reserved to allow argument or a quarrel.

They spent the first fifteen years of matrimony not at East Croydon but at Stanmore. The bank had offered Arthur a better post at the branch there, and Margaret urged him to accept it: she had not returned to work after her foreign travels.

They rented accommodation, visited their respective widowed mothers in East Croydon at weekends, and lived their humdrum lives, Arthur busily at the bank and Margaret doing odd secretarial jobs.

Ironically, a matter of months before his mother passed on, the bank appointed Arthur to an Assistant Managership back in his hometown. He was glad, Margaret was gladder, and she resumed her pre-marital work for Malcolm Barratt and his partners in the dental practice. They moved into the family house of generations of East Croydon Pendles.

Almost immediately, believe it or not, Arthur fell in love. Still stranger to relate, his love at first sight for one of his cashiers, Barbara Kent, who was equally middle-aged, married too, and with three children, was reciprocated.

Seated side by side in the Ledger Room the first time they were alone together, they blushed, trembled, held hands, kissed or nuzzled, laughed, cried, and gazed at each other happily and helplessly through their spectacles.

Barbara Kent was nowhere near so pretty as Margaret Pendle. Barbara had a nice homely face and a comfortable figure, whereas Margaret had retained the glossy look and the svelte outline of youth. Yet Barbara, paradoxically and belatedly, introduced romance into Arthur's life: in her eyes he was a hero as well as her true mate, lord and master. She regarded him with none of Margaret's cool objectivity, and was much more physically responsive.

There was never any question in Arthur's mind of breaking up Barbara's marriage or his own: her pleading with him not to force her to abandon her husband Chris and her children was superfluous. They agreed to keep their secret, and expressed confidence in each other's discretion.

Arthur, to begin with, suffered from guilt, and was concerned in case Margaret should detect his adultery and be hurt. But shortly after he had begun to betray his wife she paid him a rare and reassuring compliment: 'Arthur, it does me good to see you in such fine fettle.' This remark, combined with his irrepressible happiness, covered a multitude of sins.

Actually, East Croydon seemed to suit both Pendles

for one reason and another. Margaret enjoyed her work for Malcolm Barratt, and was pleased to be living closer to her mother. She was turning into an increasingly dutiful daughter, and would call on her mother on most evenings, then have to hurry home pink-cheeked to cook supper for Arthur, apologising for her lateness and thanking him for his patience, not knowing that he had probably seized the opportunity to spend a little extra time with Barbara.

The lovers' meetings outside banking hours, unsheltered by the bank, were difficult to arrange and dangerous. Once a week or maybe once a fortnight, Chris Kent, who was in insurance, would offer or be prevailed upon to take the Kent children to their extra-curricular evening classes; then Arthur and Barbara might dare to drive in separate cars to a sequestered countrified spot and walk in the woods in dry weather, or sit and cuddle in one car when it was cold or wet.

Intimacy, as policemen used to call it, did not occur until they had been involved for six months. They grew frustrated not only because they were impatient to consummate their love; also because Arthur had not been granted his marital rights for ages, indeed Margaret had banished him to sleep in a dressing-room, and Barbara was starved of sexual satisfaction by Chris. One moonlit spring evening they did the deed in the open air under an oak tree. Like everything else in their joint experience, it was perfect.

Time passed again, a year, five, ten, fifteen more years.

There had been changes, but not in a relevant sense. Arthur Pendle was well-preserved in his late fifties, his cap of straight flat hair was scarcely grey; but he had added dignity to his resemblance to Mickey Mouse.

146

Margaret Pendle was still shapely, but had dyed her hair red-blonde. Barbara was white-haired now, but her face was remarkably unlined and behind her spectacles her eyes were calm and fulfilled.

The three Kent children grew up and left home. Sometimes Chris, who was doing better in his career, was despatched on business trips to the USA. And Margaret Pendle took to staying a couple of nights a week in her aged mother's house. Therefore Arthur had chances, which were not missed, even to sleep with Barbara in her home or in his.

Their love had been authenticated by its durability, and reinforced by having had to be resourceful. Sometimes the lovers dreamed together and separately of might-have-beens, the joys that might have been theirs if they had met when they were young and single. But they were grateful rather than greedy. They mainly thanked their lucky stars for the unexpected bonus of their affinity and communion.

That communion was the more joyful for not being selfish: at least Arthur and Barbara had succeeded in keeping the secret of their love affair from their spouses, who had never complained about it and really had no reason to. Chris Kent got all he seemed to need from Barbara, and their children likewise. Margaret Pendle had continued to flourish throughout the period in question, apart from the year or two after her boss's wife ran off with another member of the dental practice: she had suffered from the strain of having to console and support Malcolm Barratt, and from the fear that she was going to lose a congenial job.

Predictably, the happiness of the four interested parties was too good to last – or to last any longer.

One morning at the bank Barbara fainted. When she recovered consciousness and was well enough, Arthur volunteered to drive her home. In the car she told him that Chris had been offered a highly-paid partnership in an insurance company in America.

She was extremely distressed, said she could not and would not go to live in the USA, she could not be parted from the man she loved, and she was prepared to tell Chris everything and let him divorce her, let him emigrate on his own, let him be lonely in a strange country, while she stayed put and near Arthur.

Arthur for his part, his own distress notwithstanding, grasped the points that the Kents' divorce and attendant publicity would jeopardise his marriage; that the truth would probably shatter and destroy Margaret, who had believed his countless lies; that Chris would be at risk for the same reason; and that the results of drastic action, revelations and so on, were likely to be nothing gained, every cause lost, and everybody miserable.

He therefore counselled second and third thoughts, although he too pined to liberate their love.

The very next day Margaret Pendle's mother expired. She had been very old and ill; but her daughter took her death terribly to heart.

And the day after that Arthur called Barbara into his office as the bank was closing. They both looked ten years older, they drooped unhealthily and tragically. He explained about his mother-in-law and said: 'I must help Margaret, and you must help Chris,' and Barbara said: 'I know,' and they parted for ever.

Arthur endured his life without Barbara at the bank and in East Croydon for six months. Then he blurted out to Margaret that he was retiring, he wanted her to pack in her job, and they would remove to somewhere on the sunnier south coast.

Her response was again hysterical. He apologised for upsetting her, but insisted that he meant to implement his plan with or without her cooperation: he was at the end of his tether and felt he had to.

In due course she agreed to do as he said. She made a tearful formal speech of capitulation to the effect that she wished to repay him for having been such a good, patient, loyal, indulgent and forbearing husband.

So they arrived in Brighton, and began to tell each other the tale that their flat in Kemptown was lovely, their enforced leisure was a relief, their new impressions were stimulating, and they did not miss East Croydon.

Nevertheless her favourite pastime was to sit staring out to sea and chain-smoking on their glassed-in balcony, and they both lost weight steadily.

Margaret's death from lung cancer was quick at any rate. She was admitted to hospital the day it was diagnosed and dead a fortnight later. Luckily she seemed to be unaware of what was happening to her and spoke of recovering right up to the end.

Arthur was faced with the task of disposing of her clothes. At the back of the cupboard in her bedroom he found an attaché case full of letters. He could not resist reading one, and finally, sick at heart, read the lot.

They were all signed M, obviously for Malcolm Barratt, who must have not only employed, also seduced, Margaret forty-odd years before: for she became pregnant, had to go abroad to have an abortion, and at her mother's instigation broke off the adulterous relationship. She married Arthur on the rebound and again to please her mother, but could not give him much love or, for that matter, thanks to the abortion, a baby. Malcolm had corresponded with Margaret throughout the Pendles' sojourn in Stanmore; and as soon as they returned to East Croydon she had again become his receptionist and mistress. No – it was not Margaret's proximity to her mother that put the roses in her cheeks, any more than it was the air of East Croydon that accounted for the fineness of Arthur's fettle: they were in good health and spirits at this time because they were both in love. A hundred and more treasured notes referred to assignations during the hours which Margaret was supposed to have spent with her mother.

The rest of the story was easy to piece together. Margaret had her first breakdown because Malcolm had been deserted by his wife and was begging Margaret to desert her husband, because, in other words, she was torn between doing what she wanted to do for and with the man she loved and not doing what she believed would fatally wound the man she was married to. And her second and last breakdown, and the onset of her incurable wretchedness, could be traced to the same source, the division of her loyalties because Arthur wanted to take her to Brighton and Malcolm wanted her not to be taken – taken away from him.

But she had again opted for her husband. The death of her mother had influenced her decision, since it had robbed her of a reason and an excuse to spend time with her lover. Margaret must have rejected or been rejected by Malcolm in the end: for the correspondence seemed to terminate with her departure from East Croydon.

Arthur, reading it, suffered a succession of emotions: astonishment; some resentment and embarrassment over

150

having been such a fool, and so fooled; pity and self-pity; and a lot of regret.

If only he had known! If only they had! He would have been happy to hand Margaret over to Malcolm – all three of them trapped within that eternal triangle would have been happier, and the same probably applied in the other triangular context, notwithstanding the undefined attitude of Chris.

Arthur, pining and yearning for Barbara, grieving over Margaret, alone and under-nourished in the alien Kemptown flat, could put up no resistance to such bitter and futile reflections.

He fell ill and in hospital cried deliriously: 'Waste, waste!'

His recovery was unwelcome, therefore slow, and dogged by the negative wish that everybody involved in the drama of his past had been less conventional and cowardly, less considerate of one another, less moral and good, and more committed, honest, selfish, wicked.

He had been a practical man, a man of action in a mild way, neither philosophical nor religious. He had never pondered his attitude to, or prepared his defences against, the destructiveness of fate. He could see no straw of a personal theoretical kind to clutch at, and believed, and even began to wish, that his uncharacteristically negative vision of existence would be the death of him too.

Paradoxically, in time, and perhaps in a somewhat exaggerated manner of speaking, he was rescued by repetition of that other hopeless phrase, 'If only we had known!'

None of them had known when it mattered, Barbara and Malcolm still did not know, Margaret perhaps never would know in a worldly sense, he repeated; and who knows whether knowing would have solved their problems, as he imagined. Who knows anything? He had not known, and never would have guessed, that he was destined to fall in love with Barbara, and that their adulterous liaison would last so long and be without blemish.

Extraordinary, wonderful, unknowable things did sometimes happen – he could vouch for it.

Of course death was an unknowable thing; poor Margaret had died unexpectedly, and he himself had almost followed suit; dying and pain and sorrow came out of the blue; his marriage of many years had ended in a matter of days and the love of his life in hours; and he might give up the ghost at any moment, or else continue to cry over spilt milk.

But there were alternatives: some new interest might grow out of some old one, circumstances might reunite him with Barbara. Although such scenarios, unlike death and decay, were uncertain, they were possible even at this late stage.

The point was, the truth was, the saving grace for Arthur Pendle was the platitude: 'You never know.'

An Actress's Life for Me

WHAT DO YOU want to be when you grow up, Laura?'
   'An actress, Uncle.'
'You're a brave girl.'

'Laura, here's your report from school.'
   'Yawn yawn.'
   'It's not right to take that attitude. Your mother and I are paying a lot of money to get you educated. And your headmistress says that you show no interest in learning anything. You might try a bit harder.'
   'Oh Daddy!'
   'You're not the one with reason to complain.'
   'But you know – so does Miss Barstow – that I am interested in something.'
   'Listen, you've been told acting isn't likely to get you very far. I wish you wouldn't waste so much of your time on theatricals.'
   'But I thought you liked the way I act. You and Mummy always say you like my performances in school plays.'
   'We do like them, darling. But that's not to say to

153

hell with your education. Everybody needs qualifications nowadays.'

'You're such a philistine, Daddy.'

'Your mother and I worry about you.'

'Silly old Daddy.'

'What's wrong, Loll?'

'Parents!'

'What are they doing to you now?'

'Fussing, as per.'

'Hard cheese, Lolly.'

'I'll show them. I'll show everyone. You wait, Peg!'

'My darling Laura's turning into a beautiful butterfly.'

'Was I a caterpillar when you saw me last, Uncle?'

'Yes, a little wriggly caterpillar.'

'I'm going to be sixteen.'

'Congratulations! And still set on becoming an actress?'

'Absolutely! I know the lines of Juliet, Ophelia, Desdemona and Rosalind by heart.'

'I hope you realise your ambitions without losing your illusions.'

'Oh Uncle, please don't you try to discourage me!'

'I won't if you promise me never to lower your standards.'

*

'Mummy?'

'Yes?'

'Will you let me audition for this part in a new film by Jix Palinovsky?'

'Who?'

'Jix Palinovsky – he directed *Chocolate Drops* and *The Blowfly* – he's brilliant.'

'Judging by his name he can't be English.'

'What difference does that make?'

'Don't you want to act on the stage?'

'The audition is on a stage. It's in a club theatre in London called The Den. And a film would be practice for me. Honestly, Mum, there's no harm in it – hundreds of other girls will be auditioning – and I'm seventeen and I won't even get the part.'

'I suppose I could take you.'

'Oh no! I'd be paralysed with nerves if you were watching. I promise to be good and careful on my own.'

'And meanwhile you'll twist your father round your little finger whatever I say.'

'Are you telling me I can go? Thank you so much!'

'All right, all right.'

'I love you best, Tony.'

'Do you know how much I love you, Laura?'

'I think I do.'

'Next Saturday evening my parents are staying with friends – we could have the whole house to ourselves.'

'Oh Tony!'

'I've never been with anybody else. I'd take precautions, and everything. But I don't want to force you.'

'You wouldn't have to. But please let's wait. I feel too young. I don't feel ready. And I've got this audition.'

'Exactly – you're old enough to be a film star.'

'I'm not a film star yet, and probably never will be. And I don't want to be mean. I love you so. But my career means such an awful lot to me, Tony. I feel I must hold back, and keep pure, and give myself to my acting. It's like dedication, or becoming a nun. Can you understand?'

'Nuns don't kiss boys.'

'Well – not a nun in that case.'

'Thank goodness you're safely home, Laura.'

'Hullo, Daddy, hullo, Mum. Nothing much happened. We hung around all day. I was only on stage for about two minutes. Is there anything to eat?'

'Your dinner's in the oven. I'll get it for you.'

'Weren't they pleased with you, sweetie?'

'I've no idea, Dad. The last thing they wanted to hear about was the quality of mercy. There were lots of professional actresses there, singing and tap-dancing.'

'Are you disappointed?'

'Not really. I'm glad I've done it.'

'Come into the kitchen, Laura.'

'Peg?'

'Lolly! Tell!'

156

'They made me undress.'

'No!'

'They wanted me to take my dress off. They were sitting in the stalls in the dark in this squalid theatre.'

'While you did Portia in the nude?'

'They interrupted after the first few sentences. Peg, swear you'll never split on me? My parents would die if they knew.'

'Cross my heart. What was Jix Palinovsky like?'

'I never met him. I met no one important. They were sort of shadowy, four or five of them sitting in the theatre and staring. Some woman gave the orders. 'Would you mind removing your dress? Turn right, please. Turn your back, please.'

'Did you have anything on underneath?'

'Bra and panties. I couldn't have done it otherwise. But a few of the girls took off their underwear on purpose. They said they'd do anything to get into films.'

'Would you?'

'I don't know.'

'It was only one little audition, Tony, I spoke about a third of Portia's speech in *The Merchant of Venice*, then I hurried home – what's wrong with that? My parents let me do it. No, I haven't seen Palinovsky's movies, but nor have you – I don't believe they're pretentious porn – everybody says they're terrific works of art. He's going to film an up-to-date version of *Miss Julie* by August Strindberg – it's a classic play – it's perfectly respectable. Oh Tony, you don't need to be jealous. I won't get the

part – don't worry! And I don't like it when you're suspicious and cynical.'

'There's a letter for you, Laura.'
  'Mum, I don't dare open it.'
  'Shall I?'
  'It'll only say nothing doing.'
  'You're wrong – it's an offer – let's see.'
  'Oh no!'
  'Congratulations – your father's going to be proud as
punch.'

'We're both so proud of you, darling.'
  'Thanks, Daddy.'
  'I always knew you were a better actress than the rest
of them put together.'
  'What do I do now, Dad?'
  'Your mother told me you're taking a long hard look
at the future. You're right to be cautious, and not to rush
to accept the first of the many offers you're going to
receive. But there can't be much harm in letting this agent
chappie come and talk to us, as Mr Palinovsky suggests.
Don't you agree?'
  'Yes.'
  'There might be quite important money involved. I'll
help you to write a reply to Mr Palinovsky's letter, if you
like.'
  'Would you?'

'Aren't you excited, sweetie?'
'Yes.'

'Gosh, Loll, I wish I was in your shoes. In fact, if I was in your shoes I wouldn't mind taking them off.'
 'Not funny, Peg.'

'Why did you have to say that? The casting couch was not where I got the job. Why do you drag sex into everything? It makes me sad. We ought to trust each other. No, Tony, honestly, I hate it. And I'm not kissing and making up – sorry!'

'Laura, sit down, listen and keep your head screwed on very tight. We've got ten minutes to make up our minds before Mr Woolf comes back with the contracts for you to sign or not to sign. Here are my notes of what's actually on offer. Jix Palinovsky's willing to pay you twenty-five thousand pounds for acting Miss Julie and for renewable options on your playing parts in his next films. Mr Woolf has negotiated these terms with Jix and is prepared to act as your agent for a fee of fifteen per cent plus expenses. The main trouble is that Jix will be ready to start work – shooting, I should say – in a fortnight, so we have to take our decision now or never.'
 'Oh Dad!'
 'The safeguards are that the contracts are common-or-

159

garden legal forms, nothing special or fishy; and as a rule options can be wriggled out of; and your arrangements with Mr Woolf would be for no more than twelve months to begin with.'

'Do you like him, Dad?'

'Don't you?'

'His name's sinister.'

'Maybe. But I think he's straight and quite pleasant. He's got letters after his name, he belongs to professional institutions, so he wouldn't wish to blot his copybook. And then he knows and is recommended by Palinovsky, which should be advantageous from your point of view.'

'Can I speak to Mum?'

'What's the matter, sweetie?'

'I'm frightened.'

'Oh – well – I suppose you would be. But remember that twenty-five thousand pounds for a few weeks' work is more money than your mother and I between us earn in a year. The opportunity's golden, and my advice is for pity's sake don't miss it.'

'What am I to do?'

'You were determined to be an actress, Laura. You were determined to take part in the audition. Isn't it a little late to change your mind?'

'Mum, please!'

'If you want my opinion for once, why rush? Because you've had this offer you're bound to get others. You haven't been too happy lately, and I thought you were right not to want to hurry into anything.'

'Are you telling me to refuse to sign on?'

160

'Good gracious no! Your father would kill me if I told you that. He believes the money would give you independence and security. It's up to you, dear. You've reached the age when it always is.'

'Goodbye, Peg – I leave for London tomorrow.'

'Are you looking forward to becoming a big star overnight?'

'I certainly am.'

'Lucky Lolly!'

'Yes.'

'So why can't I hear you jumping for joy?'

'Sorry – I mustn't grumble. But Mum, who was always okay about my acting, turned against my doing this job. And then Dad, who's been against my acting all along, more or less forced me to do it. Everything's been such a hectic muddle. I'm not sure I've taken the right decision.'

'What have you got to lose, except your virtue? They're not going to kill you, are they?'

'I'll let you know. Peg, I'm afraid I've half-broken up with Tony – don't let him forget me.'

'I won't. Where are you living in London?'

'With my uncle, which is great. Here's his telephone number.'

'Laura, what's the matter, why are you crying?'

'I can't, Uncle – it was terrible – and everyone was angry with me – I can't go on – and they say I can't get out!'

'Tell me, darling.'

'I can't – it's so embarrassing – it was so embarrassing, Uncle!'

'Is it a sex film?'

'Sort of – when I clocked in at The Den this morning, they took me straight to a dressing-room where the make-up people told me to strip completely. I couldn't, I wouldn't, and Mr Woolf threatened to ruin Daddy with all the penalty clauses in my contract, and Jix Palinovsky raged at me for being a virgin, and I don't know what else.'

'Here's my handkerchief, and I'll fetch you a drop of brandy.'

'Oh no, Uncle, please – no more brandy! And I'm so sorry, Uncle, because I gave in and broke my promise to you.'

'If you'd really broken it and lowered your standards, you wouldn't be crying now.'

'It's such a relief to cry. They made me do this terrible scene with Miss Julie's terrible lover – he's a footman called Jean in the play – I don't even know his actual name – in front of all the people and over and over again. And I'll have to go on doing it for days and even weeks. And it'll be exhibited in cinemas and on television.'

'You wanted to be an actress, Laura.'

'Yes, I did – I do want to act fine interesting women and speak moving lines – not to mime pornography. They say it's art and modern, but it's just attracting attention by hook or crook, and causing a sensation, and making money in the cheapest easiest way. And for me it's blackmail.'

'Where are your contracts?'

'At home – but we couldn't ask for them – Dad mustn't

know he made a mistake in advising me to sign on the dotted lines. Anyway, it wasn't his fault – I had a rough idea of what I was in for – but not the nerve to back out. Forgive me, Uncle – I'll be better in a minute – I can't go on crying, I'll look so hideous tomorrow.'

'Do you mean to return to work?'

'Is there any alternative?'

'Mum?'

'Oh thank goodness, Laura – I thought you must have decided never to speak to us again. Didn't you receive our letters and telephone messages?'

'Are you all right, Mum?'

'What? Yes – we're all right. But how are you? Your uncle's made such a mystery of how you've been getting on.'

'I'm getting on fine. And Uncle's been so kind. Will you do me the biggest favour ever, Mum? Will you?'

'If I can, dear. What is it?'

'Don't ask me questions and stop Daddy asking them, and, above all, don't let Dad try to telephone Mr Woolf or Jix or interfere with my career.'

'Is something wrong?'

'No. Please listen carefully. I'm working hard. I must concentrate on my work. I'll talk to you properly as soon as possible. I love you – believe me – and leave me alone.'

'What's happening, Laura?'

'If you can't do me that favour, I'll have to reorganise my life and move right out of reach.'

'Oh no! I'll do it. Please don't ring off.'

*

163

'Tony, it's Laura.'

'What a surprise!'

'I'm speaking from London. How are you?'

'Okay. How are you?'

'Okay. I'm doing my film.'

'What's it like?'

'Oh – fascinating. I rang to say hullo again.'

'Hullo!'

'Are you still there, Tony?'

'Laura, I'm going out with Peggy now.'

'Oh I see. Oh Tony!'

'Should I say sorry?'

'Certainly not. Goodbye.'

'Peg?'

'Lolly! You've spoken to Tony, haven't you? We both wanted you to know. But I've been worried. Do you mind?

'Why should I, Peg? I made my choice. Are you sleeping with him?'

'Yes. Thanks for being big about it – you've set my mind at rest. How are things with you?'

'Very busy. In fact I can't stop now. I've learnt a lot at any rate. Tony's a nice person, isn't he, Peg? Nice men don't grow on trees in this neck of the woods.'

'I thought you'd have a new friend.'

'No.'

'Is the filming as bad or as good as you expected?'

'It's okay. I must stop. Goodbye, Peg.'

*

'Sweetie, I couldn't resist trying to have a word with you, although I gather you don't want to be bothered while you're working so hard.'

'Dad!'

'I'm sorry, sweetie, but I do miss you.'

'Same here.'

'When am I going to see you?'

'As soon as ever I can. Are you well, Dad?'

'Not bad. And you? You're not ill or unhappy, are you?'

'Oh no – the opposite.'

'I can't wait for your film.'

'We'll have to talk about that. It's not finished yet.'

'Can I help you in any way, sweetie?'

'You could send me my contracts.'

'Are you in trouble?'

'No, no! Just send them. I'm so sorry, Dad – I've got an appointment.'

'Uncle, can you spare a moment?'

'Yes, darling.'

'I'm moving out of your lovely house, I've rented a tiny flatlet, I can afford it now, and I want to thank you so so much for seeing me through these last weeks.'

'I don't like to think of you on your own, Laura.'

'I'll be better alone. I feel too soiled and ashamed to meet people, especially people from the past. I won't do anything stupid.'

'How do you see your way ahead?'

'The options in my contracts can't be wriggled out of. Poor actresses either starve or do whatever they're told

165

to do by dirty old directors. But Jix has to pay me; and even though Mr Woolf takes a huge slice of my earnings for doing nothing, except browbeating me, one day I'll have enough money to be able to stand up for myself and say no.'

'You're too young, and too sensitive and romantic, to be mixed up in this business.'

'Perhaps I was too young. And I have thought I was too sensitive. But now I've come round to thinking I'm pretty normal and the people I work with and for are the abnormal ones.'

'Your prettiness is your handicap. Are you pestered by men?'

'Yes.'

'And not in love with anyone who might protect you?'

'I used to be long ago – three months ago – but my priorities came between us – I left him and lost him – and now what I have to pretend to do puts me off ever really doing it.'

'Yet real true love changes everything, they tell me.'

'I wish I could change so as to be able to look Mum and Dad in the eye again. The trouble is that if my film does well I'll never live it down.'

'Regret nothing.'

'Oh Uncle! I'll try not to have regrets. And I'll try to make the ugliness of my acting a little bit beautiful. But I wonder if I can.'

'Trying and wondering is how to succeed.'

The Plays of Pete Ickles

P ETE ICKLES, the left-wing playwright and propa-
gandist, sat at a desk with a blank sheet of paper
in front of him and his head in his hands in the
Ritz Hotel.

His National Health spectacles lay on the desk. He
could not see without them. He could not write without
them. But anyway he could not write. He felt trapped
and desperate, sitting in the softly upholstered chair in
the luxurious and expensive bedroom.

Pete Ickles was thirty-nine years of age. He was a York-
shireman, born and brought up in the village of Coalsley,
near Skipburgh. His father had been a miner, but was
involved in an accident down the mine in his thirties and
pensioned off, and died at fifty-five. His mother was an
ex-domestic servant, who had earned an extra penny by
taking in washing and sewing. She still lived at Coalsley
with her two unmarried daughters, Queenie and May, in
the bigger house Pete had bought her – her other older
daughters, Ada and Margaret, were married. Pete was
the youngest of the five Ickles children; with their parents
they had once crammed into a rented two-bedroomed
terrace-cottage in Hill Parade.

Not only because he was the baby of the family, also
because even in infancy he was obviously bright, Pete
received preferential treatment from his mother. Ethel

Ickles at the time in question was a red-handed sharp-nosed tight-fisted and dominating woman, quietly resentful of the hardness of her life. In her little boy, who could speak and then read at a much earlier age than the girls, she saw the possibility of the realisation of latent ambitions. She dreamed of him going to university, like the sons of the gentry she had worked for, and of herself transfigured by reflected glory.

Pete received better food and more maternal attention than his siblings. He was coached with his lessons in the parlour, while they had to sit in the kitchen. The wherewithal was begged and borrowed to send him to a private educational establishment in Skipburgh before he got into the Grammar School. When he was eleven he was removed from the bottom of the bed shared by Ada and Margaret and allowed to sleep alone on the parlour settee. The volume controls on the radio and record-player had to be turned down during his hours of homework; and his sisters in jealous fits called him St Peter.

Their father, Stanley Ickles, lamed by his accident and in pain, nonetheless cheerful and patient, would explain: 'Pete's doing his best to repay our little sacrifices. He's doing well, he's our pride now and maybe in future, not that we've cause to be ashamed. No! Our Pete's earned his chances. He's got more grey matter than the rest of us put together. Whether or not it'll make a happy man of him, that's a different question.'

All the children loved philosophic Stan Ickles. The girls had smiles for him and hugged him, and Pete until he was nine or ten followed him everywhere like a dog. But in due course Stan was unable to answer his son's increasingly precocious questions, or gave wrong and disillusioning replies. Then he complicated the issue by suddenly dying.

Changes ensued. Without his pension the family was poorer, and still more so when Ada and Margaret left home to marry the young men they had been walking out with. Queenie and May were withdrawn from school at the earliest opportunity in order to help with the laundry. And Ethel Ickles, widowed, untrammelled by matrimony, skimped and saved and worked her fingers to the bone for the sake of Pete, who was soon made ill by the additional pressure as it were to provide value for money.

His road to recovery – to Damascus, almost – was signposted by the single word: socialism.

Radical thinking had been part of his history lessons. Traditionally the Ickles family voted Labour, and Coalsley leant to the left. The difference for Pete was that he perceived the relevance, the applicability, of political theory and practical politics to his personal predicament.

Socialism seemed to solve his every problem. Why had his dear departed father suffered so much and died so young? – Because he was victimised by capitalist forces. Why had Stan Ickles been ignorant? – Because he had never received the education which was a human right. Why resigned to his pitiful lot? – Because his spirit was broken by economic injustice. And why were most people enslaved by poverty? – Because they were on the losing side in the class war for the time being.

Pete was not very popular at school. He was too clever at work, too stupid at games, and too ugly. His specs magnified his eyes, his complexion was pasty, he had jowls already, and his skull rose to a peculiar peak at the back. Yet his character under that unprepossessing exterior was generous and affectionate and honest. His

169

sisters acknowledged it: they called him St Peter because he was good in their opinion as well as being infuriatingly perfect in their mother's.

Socialism was the means by which intelligence and compassion could reform the system, rescue the deserving masses, and win their love – or so Pete believed. He rose from his bed of sickness refreshed, and altruistically raging against the past and present conditions of existence at 2 Hill Parade, the work-worn hands of his mother, the servitude of his sisters, the exploitation that was another name for profit, the cruelty of laws made by the upper class, the confidence trick of religion, and all the other Aunt Sallies of the socialist conscience.

His illness could be compared to a sort of cocoon. The merest caterpillar, grubbing round for marks at school, worn out by selfish competition, had sought refuge in it, and now an ideologically beautiful butterfly, committed to saving the world, to pacifism, republicanism, iconoclasm in general, and to the new improved socialist order, emerged. His swotting was legitimised, and his unpopularity would be rendered temporary, by his ideals and aims.

To put it another way, he had crossed the usual rubicon between boyhood and youth, and found himself in socialist rather than sexual territory.

Pete Ickles won a scholarship to Shelbrigg University and lodged in a house in York Street in the town. He was expected to carry off the highest academic honours and had already been approached by a recruiting officer for the Civil Service.

But neither in that promised land of academe, nor at home, despite the applause he received there, was he as happy, as militantly positive and optimistic, as a crusading socialist should be.

He was disconcerted and confused by the behaviour of his family. Briefly, and to begin with, his sister Ada's husband, the former Coalsley butcher locally known as Porky Pat, sold his business premises to a property developer for a considerable sum of money; and at the same time Margaret's husband, the builder and decorator Glen, threw in his lot with a bigger firm and was much better off. Then Pat and Glen pooled their resources in order to buy, let and sell houses – they became landlords with bulging bank accounts and uncharitable reputations in the neighbourhood.

Some of this relative wealth was funnelled back via Ada and Margaret to the Ickles house in Hill Parade. Gains ill-gotten by socialistic standards, humiliating handouts and bribes in Pete's terminology, were accepted gladly by his poor mother and his spinster sisters, and, he suspected, secretly used to subsidise his studies. When he spoke of the workers of the world standing shoulder to shoulder, spurning bourgeois values and the consumer society, Queenie and May told him to grow up, and Mrs Ickles assured him that one day he would be making as much money as anybody.

How could his mother so misunderstand his motives? How could she be, and believe he was, so materialistic?

On the other hand, how could he deny his nearest and dearest the comfort of a little additional cash?

The connected questions at the back of his mind, which he hardly dared formulate, were: had he already been corrupted by the middle-class money in the form of

171

scholarships, bursaries, grants and loans of which he was in receipt? Was he betraying socialism by qualifying himself for top jobs and their obscene levels of remuneration?

In the latest of last analyses, who was right, himself or the rest of his family doing what seemed to come naturally?

Pete's anxieties were exacerbated by his feelings for Janet Ellis-Mott.

Shelbrigg was a new university, its halls of residence were still being built, and meanwhile many under-graduates had to live in private rented accommodation. Moreover Shelbrigg was not only co-educational, but, despite the protests of parents who feared they would have to cope with unwanted pregnancies and so on, re-fused to take into account the sex of the undergraduates they shut up together in the same house.

Pete was allocated the ground floor front room, Janet the room on the upper floor of 10 York Street, Shelbrigg, while the landlord and landlady lurked in the basement. A couple of hours after clocking in on the first day of their first term they almost collided on the landing where the bathroom was located: she was coming out, he was trying to get in.

She said, 'I'm Jan.'

He said: 'Oh hullo.'

And he began to brood about her.

He was nineteen and a sexual ignoramus. He was not even sure if he had reached the age of puberty: he had been too busy. He had taken virtually no interest in his sisters' physiques, functions, faculties and girlish conver-sations.

But the proximity of a young female he was not related

to, and their isolation in strange surroundings, put a spark to his dry imagination. He took to lingering in the bathroom after she had been there. He was intrigued by items of her underwear he discovered on the towel-rail. He wove amorous fantasies in his solitude.

She was a tall square-shouldered flat-chested scowling girl with straight mousey hair and a pudding-basin haircut. Her charm for him was partly her plainness: if she had been prettier he might not have presumed to entertain thoughts of making love to her. And she dressed poorer than he did: always in down-at-heel pirate boots, ragged jeans and threadbare sloppy-joe sweaters.

Notwithstanding these reassuring factors, he could not summon the courage to speak to her. Equally, although she left her laundry lying about for him to find, like *billets-doux*, she must have avoided him. Somehow, between them, they managed not to meet properly for a month or so, although they were living under the same roof and both had to walk from York Street to the dining-hall of their college for meals.

Then, one evening at about nine-thirty, she marched into his bed-sitting-room and demanded: 'Do you want a mug of coffee?'

He said yes and followed her upstairs to her room, where he perched nervously on the edge of her bed and she, having given him the coffee, sprawled on the floor by the gasfire.

Their conversation consisted mostly of her intrusive cross-questioning and his hesitant and mumbled replies. Was he as brainy as he looked? Was he against any sort of social life? Would he be sure to wash the bath after shaving in it? When he denied that he was a recluse or a hermit, she explained her forcible entry into his existence thus: 'I thought it was time we stopped playing hide-and-seek.'

Yet on another evening, when he invited her to have coffee in his bed-sitting-room, she snapped: 'Oh don't let's start all that!'

She snubbed and mystified Pete, bowled him over, tied him in knots and tempted him: an unlikely Eve with an even less likely Adam in a chill subfusc back-street apology for a Garden of Eden. Their friendship or their enmity developed through the end of that term and the beginning of the next as and when she pleased. If he should enter her room without knocking, or take anything for granted, she railed at him. She refused his invitations to drink his coffee, or accompany him to their college for supper, almost on principle. But her demands for his company were peremptory; and if he dared to follow her example and say he was otherwise engaged, she would call him boring – 'You're just incredibly boring!'

She had no respect for him. In good moods she called him her 'ickle chum', in bad moods 'Mole!' Referring to his academic success, she said he knew everything that did not matter. But disrespect was her stock-in-trade. She was sceptical and scornful, and seemed to believe in nothing, apart from a certain stoical self-reliance. She was reading Sociology and he was reading History at Shelbrigg: she said both subjects were high-faluting nonsense, and that their university was a second-rate dump. When she had flu and a fever, she battled through her daily round; when she gave it to him and he retired to bed, she said he was soft.

She guessed that he had a strong-minded mother behind him, and older sisters. 'They've spoilt you,' she

174

told Pete, who had liked to think of himself as a representative of the disadvantaged and under-privileged classes. She would have turned other ideas of his upside down, if he had not regarded her criticism as mere tactics in the sex war. She was interested in his background: he re-lived his life in story-form for her amusement. But when he came to his conversion to socialism she jeered 'How corny!' – and explained further: 'Poor boy decrees that no one shall be rich – you're so predictable!' What were her politics, he asked with unwonted testiness. She said she was a socialist too – 'a National Socialist, like Hitler'.

Her customary response to questions appertaining to her own parentage, home, childhood and youth was to pretend to yawn. Sometimes she would deign to say she was at Shelbrigg precisely to forget who she was and where she came from. Pete deduced from her twangy vowel sounds, and laughter at and mimicry of his Yorkshire accent, that she hailed from the snobbish south.

Throughout the second half of their second term at York Street, the Easter term, they spent time together at her behest pretty well every day. Towards the end of the period in question the early spring weather turned nasty, and one evening Jan complained to Pete, walking back to their lodgings after supper in College, that she was perishing of the cold. She was frozen out of doors and indoors too, in her bed-sitter, she said, where the gasfire was inadequate and the draughts blew her bedclothes off at night. Shelbrigg was a miserable hole, she continued, and its university was no better, and she was learning nothing about anything, and was sorry she had ever set foot in Yorkshire.

She was slouching along beside Pete in a filthy old donkey-jacket she had bought in a charity shop.

175

He said, trying to cheer her up: 'When I was a lad I thought Shelbrigg was the hub of the universe.'

'That's what was wrong with you then, and still is,' she retorted.

He laughed and objected mildly: 'You're not very nice to me, you know,' and on a foolhardy impulse he plucked at her arm as if to comfort her – she had her hands in her jacket pockets.

She shrugged away at once and violently, saying: 'Don't make us look any more ridiculous than we do already!'

He was startled, hurt by her reactions to his first physical overture, and enquired: 'Do you think we look ridiculous?'

'Do you think you don't?' she countered savagely.

He was silenced.

In the hall of 10 York Street she said: 'Oh come on – you can have a cup of my best coffee,' and upstairs, ten minutes later, referring to the coffee: 'I'm drinking mine in bed – sorry, but I want to try to get warm.'

Whereupon she quickly undressed, except for her knickers, and climbed into bed, while he, sitting on the only chair in the room, stared and blushed.

She pulled the covers up to her chin – she had anyway shown Pete no more of her skinny tense figure than many girls show on crowded summer beaches.

She laughed and challenged him: 'Go down to your room if I've frightened you.'

He gazed at her through his thick spectacles, gauchely shook his pointed head, murmured 'No!' in a thick voice, and aimed a wobbly smile in her direction.

'Poor ickle Pete,' she mocked him. 'Why don't you drink your coffee and join me?'

176

'I will if you're not careful,' he managed to reply.

She drank from her mug, put it down on the floor, turned on her side with her back to him and said: 'I wish you'd switch out the light whatever you decide to do – I'm sleepy.'

He felt wretched, in a dilemma and the opposite of libidinous; but at last he did take off his glasses and his clothes in the dark and stumbled blindly towards the bed and got in beside her.

The strangest act of love ensued. When she stopped shivering and he stopped trembling, she really seemed to sleep. Their essential closeness in the narrow bed created enough warmth evidently to relax in her case and to stimulate in his. Instead of responding to his interrogative whispers of her name she snored a little, and with scarcely perceptible movements wriggled out of her knickers and shifted about in order to facilitate matters. He was finally able to achieve a consummation as awkward and partial as the rest of their relationship.

Then she woke or stirred, and exclaimed, kicking him: 'Oh God! What are you doing here? What have you done? Go away! Go!'

He argued the point in vain. She would not let him put on the light. Perhaps she cried. She certainly cursed him. He got out of her room as soon as he could, carrying most of his clothes, and in his own paced the floor, fumed, worried and felt increasingly bad. At five in the morning he collapsed on his own bed and drowsed uneasily till seven.

Jan's letter had been pushed under his door and ran as follows: 'Sorry! I've made too many mistakes – last night with you, and trying to be a student. But I didn't want

177

you to think I was just teasing. Goodbye. Good luck!
Don't pursue me.'

Pete Ickles believed his heart was broken.

But little by little he had to admit that Jan was instrumental in putting his politics together again.

Anger filled the vacuum she had left behind. Maybe he had been raw and clumsy; but she had led him on and cruelly abandoned him.

He obeyed the instruction not to pursue her with some satisfaction: he would not stoop to do so. However, on first reading her letter he failed to understand that she had decamped, he imagined she must have taken lodgings elsewhere in Shelbrigg, and therefore made enquiries at their college. He discovered that she was the daughter of The Right Honourable Sir Reginald Ellis-Mott, PC, QC, MP, a Conservative politician, who lived at Mott Park near Ashford in Kent and a flat in Westminster Gardens in London SW1, and had written to the relevant authorities to say that Janet would not be returning to the university.

He might have known. He should have known that she had been all along, and always would be, his class enemy. She had deceived him politically as well as emotionally. He felt as if he had supped with the devil without a sufficiently long spoon, or, in weaker sentimental moods, notwithstanding the absurdity of the analogy, that he and she had got entangled in a Romeo and Juliet situation. What irked and wounded him was to think that she was just a debutante taking an inquisitive peep at how the other half lives, and that her appropriation of his love was simply slumming. And he could not forgive her proven experience for shifting the blame for their sexual fiasco onto his inexperienced shoulders. She had never treated him right. She was a typical capitalist double-dealer.

How she must have laughed at him, and how, probably, she must be laughing!

Of course he had been a fool. But her clothes, poorer than any poor girl in Coalsley would be seen dead in, had misled him. Her fancy accent, which he mistook for cockney, had been transmitted by his ears to his heart rather than his head. Her secretiveness had struck him as the romantic mystery of womanhood, and, in short, love had gone and done it again and blinded him.

He was too ashamed of his folly to mention Jan to his family. At home he revelled in being hero-worshipped for a change, and not made to feel his appearance was against him. He remembered that he had managed well enough without sex, and resolved to love his people, even the people, not any person, in future.

He embraced his working-class origins, culture and habits with a new enthusiasm, wearing collarless shirts and dungarees, boots and a flat cap; rolling his own cigarettes and drinking pints of beer on principle; standing on the terraces at football matches for the first time, and so on.

At Coalsley and at Shelbrigg University he became a member of revolutionary clubs, respectively The Workers' Rights Cooperative and Revolting Students and Co., both of which were Marxist-Leninist and violently anti almost everything. Yet he soon ceased to attend meetings. He could neither breathe, see nor think in the

179

upper rooms of pubs filled with tobacco smoke and noisy argument, and in fact more than half a pint of beer made him ill.

He buried himself in his books and worked harder than ever so as to show the world that Jan had not wrecked his life and his chances, and because he believed that success would be sweet revenge, and serve his political allies and interests.

He duly won a first-class degree and returned to Coalsley, where he suffered another bout of the illness of his youth. The pressure on him to provide financial and political value for his education was counter-productive: he sank into indecision and inactivity. He did nothing for one whole year, according to his critical sisters, then for another. He turned down jobs, he would not apply for jobs, he lounged about and was bad-tempered, he even distressed his mother, and the praise of neighbours turned into blame.

Throughout this period he raged inwardly and with increasing rancour against the social system in force and the injustice of capitalism. It was intolerable, the difference made by wealth – the difficulties he and his family had had to overcome to get him where he was, and their sacrifices, compared with the frivolous carelessness of Jan's arrival at Shelbrigg University and departure. His rejection by that parasite, his inability to subdue her, the anti-climax of his graduation, which she had not responded or reacted to, and the plight of his comrades in the deprived under-classes of the wider world – all infuriated him, the more so because he bottled up his feelings and seemed to be incapable of translating them into useful action.

One day the Secretary of the Coalsley Labour Party

asked him to write something for a Christmas theatrical show at the Working Men's Club.

Pete in the course of the next three days and nights dashed off a three-act play, largely autobiographical and fraught with his ideals and obsessions, which he called: *We Want It Now.*

The Secretary of the Labour Party said it was not what he had asked for, it was too political for Christmas, and too extreme.

But the Coalsley Amateur Dramatic Society, run by a militant schoolmistress who had once taught the playwright and was proud of his intellectual attainments, put it on.

Pete cringed when he heard dialogue expressive of his deepest convictions and secrets mangled by the local talent and laughed at in the wrong places. He wished he had never written the play, and tried, if in vain, not to accept his ex-schoolmistress's proffered fee of five pounds.

Those five pounds were his first earnings. He considered that they were a tragic comment on his twenty-six years of back-breaking and spirit-breaking labour.

But the tragedy or the comedy turned out to be that his fiver was soon multiplied by a million.

We Want It Now, snowball-like, rolled on from Coalsley to Skipburgh to York to London to Broadway, gathering money, sticking more and more money to itself, and showing no signs of coming to a stop.

Pete was acclaimed and feted; gained awards, broke records; was invited to functions, asked to lecture and speechify, begged to open exhibitions, bullied by charities, forced to globetrot; and had to attend to his business affairs. He was more famous than he ever had been in his ambitious reveries, and richer than in his dreams of avarice. He had wanted it, and now he had got it. He was thrilled. He was amazed and exhausted.

The play was incredibly popular. It tickled the fancy of levellers, liberals, even curious conservatives; armchair philanthropists; guilt-ridden socialites posing as socialists, gilt-edged sensation-seekers whose flesh was made to creep; prigs, hypocrites and don't-knows; and at the same time it spoke to and for the truly dispossessed. It was grim yet optimistic: the admirable father of the hero dies as a result of an accident down the mine, but the clever hero helps the rest of the family to rise like so many phoenixes from the ashes of disaster and privation. It was saucy yet moral: the hero in boyhood sleeps at the other end of the bed he shares with two of his sisters, who put his feet to peculiar uses, but he grows up to be passionately loved by, to pity, marry and steadfastly support the woebegone blind girl he meets at university. It was full of pawky Yorkshire humour and fiery radical rhetoric.

Pete gave the money it began to earn to his mother and sisters. But by the time he had bought them the best and most modern house in Coalsley, they told him they had enough. He repaid Ada and Margaret for financial assistance in the past, and invested in the businesses of Pat and Glen; but again there were limits – Ada and Margaret did not want to be patronised by their younger brother who had pilloried them in his play – and he could not and would not buy up his brothers-in-law.

He had to engage a secretary, an agent and an accountant to deal respectively with fan-mail, contractual negotiations and tax. He needed a flat in London; he needed another in New York – they were cheaper than hotels; and cars in both countries; and clothes which would not shame him in smart places; and more telephones than he knew the numbers of; and credit cards and bank accounts galore. And every pound he was paid seemed to him a fitting reward and the overdue rectification of a sociological error. His intelligence, his years of struggle, had long merited every form of recognition.

The trouble was, the problem of his success was, that more pounds came his way than he could justify by reference to his past, his present requirements or his ideology. He was earning a living at one moment, he was comfortable and generous at the next, then he was secure, then rich, then a multi-millionaire.

At what was possibly his personal point of no return, he proposed simply to hand over his superfluity of funds to socialist organisations. But his financial advisers were against it. He would have tax to pay on the income he had already received and spent, they reminded him; and if he were to reduce his resources by so much, and if he happened to earn less in the coming months, how did he think of paying it? He was sufficiently alarmed by this argument – he did not want to go bankrupt and find himself back where he had begun. The cash in question was invested in a high yielding account, distributing hefty dividends, and thus adding to the positive flood of his revenues in the very period in which he had been advised that they might dry up.

Everything turned to gold for him. In the second year of the existence of *We Want It Now* he got a bountiful down-payment for the film rights plus a royalty on the film itself. He was still receiving a vast income from licensing performances of his play in professional theatres and by amateur groups, and for options and fees of one sort and another.

Although he had been charitable in practice as well as theory, open-handed indeed, he was now restrained not only by having to put aside the equivalent of a king's ransom to pay his annual taxes; also because he was gaining experience of confidence tricksters, the bleeding heart brigade, and pseudo-socialists who pocketed his donations to the cause and fled to capitalist islands in the sun out of reach of extradition.

Moreover he discovered that his expenditure in the name of liberality was seldom the end of the story. The property he had bought for his mother cost money to maintain; his gifts to Queenie and May gave them expectations of a higher standard of living, which he felt honour bound to provide; success committed him to that expensive luxury, a well-to-do circle of acquaintances; and his personal outgoings, the price of keeping his own show on the road, mounted steadily. He had never wanted to be quite so wealthy. But soon that want was replaced by another: he did not want to be, he could no longer afford to be, poorer. He took an increasing interest in investing his money for rainy days.

As for his sexual wants, they were slight. Sex, long ago and metaphorically, had gone to his head: his youthful passion for his books seemed to have drained him sexually. And his relationship with Jan was an off-putting cautionary tale. He was more than shy with women, he was scared of them. Nevertheless, during the run of *We Want It Now* on Broadway, the third actress to play the part of one of the hero's sisters made a dead set at him. She wore him down, she built him up – she was pretty, common, shrewd and tough. If Gloria's attitude to Pete was venal, Pete's attitude to Gloria could be called acquisitive: his money surely entitled him to every pleasure. He married her impulsively – he was excited to act out of character. In their nuptial suite, without delay, she stripped naked and said: 'You've bought it, help yourself.' He was too shocked to do so. Within a few weeks Gloria had divorced him for non-consummation of the marriage and relieved him of a cool half-million.

These legalistic facts, mortifying and embarrassing – the more embarrassing since his fame was founded upon his poverty and antagonism to the rich – were broadcast worldwide by the media. Thereafter he took steps to conceal his wealth in numbered foreign bank accounts, and he resolved never again to squander any of it on unworthy objects, for instance on deceitful girls or on gold-diggers.

A further and more subtly punitive consequence of his marriage was the commentary of Jan, when he chanced to meet her again.

He was in London; he had popped into Fortnum and Mason to do some shopping on his way to keep a theatrical appointment in the West End – he liked to shop at Fortnum's not least because he was merely one of its many famous customers. He saw a tall smart woman at the coffee counter and realised that he had shared her narrow bed nine years previously.

He would have escaped if he could.

But she turned and called out: 'It's my ickle friend!' – excitably and with a warm welcoming smile.

And physically as well as verbally she patronised him by marching across and giving him a hug.

Worse than patronage was in store. Jan praised his

play, she was full of congratulations, she said she was proud of it and of him, and then: 'It must have got your chippiness out of your system, otherwise you wouldn't be in here spending money like water with the rest of us.' She was treating him as an economic and social equal. She was assuming that he had defected from his class to apply for membership of hers, of the detestable bourgeoisie and criminal exploiters. She was taking it for granted that he had betrayed his friends and sworn allegiance to his lifelong enemies.

He asked her how she was.

'Fine,' she replied; 'married and the mother of two. Actually I was married a few weeks after walking out of that Shelbrigg dump. But I assure you my elder child doesn't look like a mole!'

She laughed and added: 'I was sorry to see your marriage came to grief. On the other hand I was glad you were able to pay the woman all that cash. You must admit it's quite nice to have money coming out of your ears. It's better than being a penniless socialist spoilsport, isn't it?'

'Goodbye, Jan,' he said.

But as usual she ignored his repressive tone, and voiced a sort of afterthought: 'By the way, are you still writing?'

'Of course.'

'Oh well . . . Goodbye, ickle Pete!'

He was deeply disturbed by this encounter. His hatred of Jan flared up again because, on top of everything else, she had made him lie about his writing. Of course, in fact, he had really not had a moment to write in the hectic years of his transmogrification from obscurity to prominence. His life had been too restless, he had too many new obligations, he could not settle to it; and he was not sure he could supply another play like *We Want It Now*, as demanded by his various agents and clamorous public.

But his socialist beliefs and ideals were intact, he assured himself: they had been reconfirmed defiantly by the scepticism of Jan. Although he was well aware that he had become a contradiction in terms and target of mockery, namely a socialist millionaire, a so-called champagne socialist, he compared his ideological position with that of good Christians who are unable to obey each and every one of the injunctions of Christ. Shopping at Fortnum's proved nothing, except that he was not an inverted snob. He was still on the side of the disadvantaged and the economic victims of people like Jan.

Consequently, a couple of years later, when the next General Election was called, Pete gave more generously than ever before of his money and his time. He wrote speeches and even made a few; but his appearance was not exactly vote-winning, and he was shyly tongue-tied by hecklers. In articles in papers he excoriated the social establishment, the upper classes, the market economy, the City of London, speculators and tax-dodgers. He was increasingly excited to think that he might be contributing to what was beginning to look like a classic victory for his beloved socialism.

But as the opinion-polls veered leftwards he had a worrying tripartite meeting with his accountant and stockbroker. He was warned that he would be relieved of a large proportion of his fortune by a socialist party in power which proposed swingeing taxation of high incomes, a capital levy and an annual wealth tax, and the recall of investments offshore; whilst the welfare programme of a socialist administration would probably reduce the value of the pound in his pocket by a considerable percentage. To safeguard his savings he signed a sort of power of attorney that allowed his advisers to take steps to minimise the damage: they mainly bought Krugerrands.

He suffered nonetheless from insomnia in the nights before Polling Day. What right had any political party, or anybody for that matter, to confiscate, to steal, the larger part of his savings? Obviously it was fair that the inherited wealth and the excessive wealth of some should be re-distributed; but he was not as wealthy as all that, he had earned every penny he possessed, and he might badly need the whole lot in the possible, if unthinkable, event of his never writing another remunerative play. How would he tell his mother and sisters that he could no longer subsidise them? How would he manage without money?

In the polling booth he hesitated; put a shaky cross beside the name of the conservative candidate; attempted in vain to rub it out and rectify his error; put a second cross beside the socialist; and, in other words, spoilt his paper.

The socialists lost the election.

Pete felt ashamed, guilty, corrupted, penitent. He had lost his way. He would go back to his beginnings. He would redeem himself. He vowed to dedicate the rest of his life and his talent to the politics of the poor.

He returned home.

It was no good. His proud old mother made too much of him, invited too many people into the house to meet

188

him, gave him no peace. His sisters and his brothers-in-law were jealous of him. The inhabitants of Coalsley who were his contemporaries resented his success, the younger ones called him sir. And everybody was after his money – local political organisations, dramatic societies, charities, individuals – while regarding him with green-eyed hostility because of it. Under the circumstances literary composition was out of the question, and he could not bury himself in a village in Yorkshire – his experience of the wider world, his interests and commitments did not permit him to.

He tried again in his flats in London and New York. He had his telephones disconnected and his meals sent in. But his writer's block did not dissolve. Middle age loomed and he continued to lose hair and teeth. And his loneliness was unbearable.

Then he spent a few nights in the Ritz Hotel in London: his flat was being re-decorated.

He arranged matters with the management of the Ritz, registered under a false name, ate in his room and emerged from it only in the middle of the night. He was looked after by the same team of servants, who were sympathetic and discreet: they allayed his fears of finding himself the subject of newspaper headlines such as Famous Socialist's Princely Lifestyle.

He was protected. He liked the luxury. He prolonged his stay and started to scribble on the hotel writing paper.

He resuscitated the plots of plays that would carry on from where *We Want It Now* left off. The true story of the autobiographical sequel, which might be entitled *I Make Millions*, would neither promote his socialist image nor meet with the approval of his socialist comrades. Yet the very idea of banging the socialist drum made his mind go blank: he simply could not do it again – his inability to produce another word of radical propaganda was like a new form of impotence. He realised his political ideas were changing, had changed, and thought of writing about a monk in the middle ages struggling to retain his faith. Unfortunately, at least for his peace of mind, he was too honest and gifted to be inspired by compromise.

And time passed. The artistic anxiety and frustration of previous years deteriorated into panic. He had sacrificed his talent, he had sold out to mammon, he saw himself as a lost soul. He refused to have dealings with the agents of his former eager materialism. Although he was spending a small fortune daily, he ceased to care whether or not he had money: he cared even less than rich people do as a rule.

Month succeeded barren month. His luxurious room became a kind of prison cell. But there was no freedom elsewhere. His feelings were similar to those he had had before *We Want It Now*, when he was incarcerated in the parlour of 2 Hill Parade, pent up and hopeless; but then he had been young, now he seemed to be past it. He was incapable of constructive cogitation. He dared not think.

So Pete Ickles despaired, and sat at a desk with a blank sheet of paper in front of him and his head in his hands in the Ritz Hotel.

He was soon to write his second play, *The Crime of This Century*, which put the blame for the horrors of the Russian revolution of 1917, the decades of mass-murder by Lenin and Stalin, the rise of Mussolini and Hitler, the holocaust, the 1939 world war, and mayhem and misery in Asia, Africa and South America, on the false premises and promises of socialism and communism.

Saying Boo to the Intelligentsia

O N SATURDAY 17 JULY 1874 Marie Bashkirtseff made the following entry in her famous diary: 'They say there are a great many rogues in Russia who want a commune, how horrible! . . . And their detestable sect is so numerous that the papers appeal to society in despair . . . They want . . . an end of civilisation, an end of art . . . Nothing but the material means for existence; universal manual labour; and no one will have the right, however great his merit, to rise above his neighbours. They wish . . . to reduce Russia to a caricature of Sparta. I hope God and the Emperor may confound their schemes.'

Maria Bashkirtseff was fourteen years of age when she wrote the above.

Her reference to Sparta is probably to the militarism and brutality of that Greek state, which produced no art.

Thus a little girl challenged the opinions, the convictions, the faith, of men who were and would be older than she was, more highly educated and qualified, more experienced, more influential.

Karl Marx, for instance, author of *The Communist Manifesto* published in 1847, was older. He spent six years at universities and emerged as a doctor of philosophy. Out of his learning and culture came the communist system, and in particular the concept of the class struggle, which he incited in his writings by means of the fierceness of his invective or the foulness of his abuse, depending on which way you looked at it. Although he was baptised a Christian in spite of his Jewish origins, he thought it was perfectly all right to set man against man.

Marx's philosophical theories were put into practice by Lenin, who played a leading part in the Russian revolution of 1917. Lenin was a lawyer turned politician. He seized power and wielded it even to the extent of breaking the laws of the land and having people punished, tortured and shot without trial, including the 'Emperor' or Tsar and his wife and their children; but excused himself on the grounds that the necessity for his 'ruthless dictatorship of the proletariat' would 'wither away'.

Meanwhile, in our own country, the torch of socialism if not communism, or, in an inclusive word, of collectivism, was borne aloft by Sidney Webb and his wealthy wife Beatrice, later Lord and Lady Passfield. They were clever enough to gain a long ascendancy over that hotbed of intellectuals, the Fabian Society, and they never tired of telling other people that they should all be equal. The Webbs travelled in the USSR in 1932, turned a blind eye to the terror-famine in the Ukraine which was in the process of doing to death fourteen million Ukrainians; and on their return published *Soviet Communism: A New Civilisation?*

At roughly the same time four clever and cultured alumni of Cambridge University were proving their support of the communist cause by agreeing to spy for Russia. Burgess, Maclean, Philby and Blunt switched their allegiance from the UK to the USSR, notwithstanding the facts that the UK was a gentle democracy and

Stalin in the USSR was now killing off his compatriots by the tens of millions.

Of course collectivism has the appeal of any utopian scheme. It promises, positively, that it can create liberty, equality, justice, a true brotherhood of man, in short heaven on earth, and, negatively, that no one will be more important or richer than you are.

Moreover power has always had its worshippers; and what could be more powerful than the power backed by the gigantic landmass of the USSR and embodied in those who ruled over it?

Top people with big brains and big mouths and either little commonsense or little principle, the blind and blinkered idealists, the opportunists wanting to be on the winning side, the defeatists of capitalism, the guilt-ridden, the envious, the controversialists and trouble-makers, vouched, proselytised, canvassed and urged their fellow-citizens of the 'freer' world to vote and to agitate for collectivism. They proclaimed that if, or rather inevitably when, collectivism got its political chance, it would be good for everyone, or at any rate for others.

Naturally poor simple-minded folk, not to mention idle and hopeless persons, were attracted to collectivism, which undertook to alleviate their suffering and gratify their every desire – and much more quickly than religions, which offered only posthumous happy-ever-after lives.

Collectivism became fashionable. The fashion, as ever, filtered down through the social pile and back up again. That the pro-collectivist attitude was a fashion is authenticated by its irrationality.

Multi-millionaires embraced collectivism and claimed

that they could hardly wait to be ruined. Dyed-in-the-wool hedonists declared that they were impatient to share the lot of Russian peasants. Aesthetes wished they were steelworkers. Churchmen embraced Marxism which mocked God. Feather-bedded western workers were all for Russian-style industrial relations that would make them work twice as hard for a fraction of the pay. Some enthusiastic female sympathisers with the cause bore communal babies.

The 1939–1945 war, and the victory of the communist form of collectivism over the fascist nazi form, seemed to justify, and certainly encouraged, the fashion-mongers. The imperialism of the USSR, which had taken over a dozen European countries, was quite different from the abhorrent imperialism of western empire-builders, they told us: it was the unstoppable tide of history, of modernism, which would shortly engulf the rest of the world. As for the disturbing rumours that were beginning to circulate about the facts of life under the red flag, and the tales told by reactionaries, the touts of communism reminded us that omelettes cannot be made without breaking eggs. Besides, they asked unanswerably, what was the alternative to the collective model of the state evolving in the USSR? Did we want to continue to grind the faces of the poor, put the working-class in its place, let the rich get richer, stick to the bad old ways, turn back the clock?

For almost the century and a half since the publication of *The Communist Manifesto*, an ever-growing proportion of the international intelligentsia peddled the 'Party line'; and millions upon millions of people in the west and the east, in Africa and South America, who respected and trusted their intellectual superiors – the communist writers, teachers, broadcasters, politicians, trade union bosses, activists and militants – in their humility and credulity bought this snake-oil panacea for their ills.

Yet nowadays, in country after country, the populace, the humble millions, Marx's proletariat and Lenin's masses raise their voices in unison; and instead of singing 'Long live collectivism', they are shouting 'Enough of it! Enough!'

Lo and behold, the natives of the USSR and of its colonies, the beneficiaries of collectivist wisdom and philanthropy, are shaking their fists at the system and even shooting and lynching its ministers.

The world we see is no longer the world we knew: it is changing kaleidoscopically.

And what are the syllables being mouthed by myriad lips, what are they crying out for?

Good gracious, they demand the very thing that the intelligentsia would not let them have, decided they were better without, derided, vilified, outlawed, made into a crime carrying the death penalty!

Yes, everybody wants to be a capitalist now.

But listen, what else are they telling us, the poorer and hungrier millions who have had experience of the Marxist version of history in action, what are they saying about the seventy-odd historic years of the full-blown collective experiment?

They are saying the class struggle was an invention of the devil: for the dividing lines between the classes, at least in most countries, can be drawn anywhere – and they were; as a result incalculable numbers of innocent people died horrible deaths, in addition to almost all the Russians who brought about the 1917 revolution. Incidentally, and ironically, members of the intelligentsia were regarded as class enemies in every fully collectivist state.

And Lenin was wrong: the dictatorships of the proletariat never withered away, they just became more and more corrupt.

And Sidney and Beatrice Webb were like those three monkeys, seeing, hearing and speaking no evil that would have interfered with their know-all collectivist theories, delivering paternalistic injunctions from on high to the rest of humanity grovelling down below.

And Burgess and company, four flowers intensively cultivated at top seats of learning, also other brainy westerners, who volunteered to betray their native lands and their friends and colleagues for the sake of the USSR and its brands of collectivism and imperialism, what did they think they were doing?

There are alternative answers: they must either have been psychopaths eager to make their contribution to Stalin's bloodbath, or, more likely, they too over-looked the available evidence, they were taken in, conned, gulled and fooled by mere propaganda.

But the survivors of collectivist regimes have still more to say about the intellectuals who believed collectivism was just the ticket.

They would take issue with two practical effects in particular of collectivist nostrums.

First, the classes of any society, classification by means of ability, merit, genealogy and inheritance, such distinctions, being natural, can be repressed by nothing but force. And that force, the essential bureaucratic terror employed in the Soviet empire, for instance, would and did destroy or at any rate inhibit all the qualities that leaven the social lump, initiative and aspiration, self-reliance and self-respect, the desires of parents to help their children, and so on. Furthermore, a 'classless' society is bound to be riddled with class-consciousness, snobbery and resentment, since it always has to offer conspicuous rewards to the bureaucrats, secret policemen and military personnel who do its forceful – or dirty – work.

Secondly, Karl Marx and his disciples denied religion because – to give them the benefit of the doubt – they believed everybody should try to do better here on earth instead of waiting passively to be scooped up to heaven. Collectivist atheists would claim that the tidings they brought, and still bring, are humanitarian: mankind must improve its one and only mundane material life. But they are inhumane, they are cruel, thus to snatch away from the ever-present poor, from the disabled and disfigured, from those dying young, from sick bodies and sad souls and frightened hearts, and from the bereaved, from that vast majority whose lives cannot be much improved, if at all, the consolation prize of resurrection and the possibility of a second chance.

Fortunately, earthbound materialism of the Marxist sort, which scoffed at the promises of religion, was counter-productive: it fostered the seed of its own destruction. For man cannot bear to live for very long, that is to say cannot bear death, without the expectation of some kind of life beyond the grave – witness the long religious history of our species, real unarguable history rather than arrogant Marxist guesswork, and the example of Christianity, which sought to complete Judaism by showing that it was possible to rise from the dead.

Therefore, at last, and thanks after all to the mercy of God, collectivism has collapsed in countries which have suffered most grievously from it, and collectivist theory has been conclusively proved erroneous in practice.

But the people or peoples emerging from the tragic mess more or less scathed have a question to ask.

How was it that a sizeable proportion of the intelligentsia of generations dating back to the middle of the nineteenth century, even intellectuals who paved the road to hell with their good intentions, failed to detect the fatal flaws in the logic of collectivism, ignored the threats and dangers inherent in its harsh dogma, affixed the seal of approval to totalitarianism, tyranny and torture, when Marie Bashkirtseff, aged fourteen, put her girlish finger on what was wrong with it and boldly condemned the whole idea?

The Law of Unintended Consequences

ANDREW PALMER WAS twelve years old and not like other boys. There was nothing wrong with him physically: he was well-made and quite nice-looking, notwithstanding his shortsightedness and his spectacles which were inclined to slip down his nose. He had a pink and white complexion, a tight cap of light brown hair with a wave in it, and a sensitive bump to the back of his head.

But his contemporaries thought he was sloppy, although most were afraid to say so in case he should furiously sulk or curse, or attack them with kicks, scratches, bites or any available blunt instrument. The charge of sloppiness derived from his attitude to our dumb friends. He literally would not hurt a fly; he bemoaned the fate of every fly that was or ever had been hurt; references to hunting, shooting or fishing reduced him to tears; and his strict vegetarianism caused infinite trouble, not least because it seemed to account for his anaemic tendency.

The Palmer family home was in Somerset. Herbert Palmer, Andrew's father, a schoolmaster by profession, had inherited a pleasant little property in the back of beyond and the wherewithal to live on it; he therefore retired early; and he and his wife Gwen were the more pleased to do so for their son and only child's sake –

199

Andrew would receive a health-giving countrified up-bringing.

However, Herbert and Gwen Palmer soon wondered if they would not have done better to stay in town. At Netherzoy House, Andrew, from the age of nine or ten onwards, not only refused all nourishing butchered food, and objected with sad insistence and persistence when it was bought, cooked, eaten and served; he was also upset by the facts of life and death on farms, and by rustic sports and pursuits. He would not play with the girls and boys with butterfly nets and catapults. And he irritated the adult community by appealing to it not to kill things. He even managed to annoy his father by begging him not to go fishing: Herbert at last advised him to stop his cheeky whining.

The senior Palmers hoped it was a phase. Andrew was compassionate, they reassured each other in optimistic moods; again, less confidently, they said Andrew was too soft-hearted; while pessimism expressed the view that over-sensitive obsessive children often grew out of their funny little ways.

Besides, he was kind to human beings as well as to animals, provided the former did not offend against his sympathies for the latter. His undestructive gentleness, if not particularly boyish, was attractive; and his anger was exclusively altruistic. He was capable of winning hearts, especially those of strangers.

The Smith-Hubbards, for instance, when they came to tea at Netherzoy House, took an immediate shine to Andrew. Mrs Smith-Hubbard, who was sixtyish and childless, liked his looks and wanted to mother him. Major Smith-Hubbard, who owned a pair of Irish wolf-hounds, was pleased to hear that they were Andrew's favourite breed of dog and by his theoretical knowledge of wolfhound characteristics.

'You'll have to meet the real live article,' Major Smith-Hubbard said. 'We call them Finn and Catty, short for Finnegan and Catriona. They're wonderful creatures, bigger than Shetland ponies, and much better behaved. Herbert,' he called to Andrew's father, 'let's fix a day when all of you can have tea with us.' He added with a somewhat chesty laugh: 'And we've a few other representatives of the animal kingdom to interest your young man.'

Herbert and Gwen Palmer exchanged a glance across the tea-table, mumbled excuses and tried to wriggle out of this invitation.

But the bluff old Major would have none of it: 'What's the problem? You name your day.' Mrs Smith-Hubbard said smilingly: 'Yes – we've got lots and lots of animals for Andrew to see.' And Andrew himself pleaded with his parents to arrange a visit to the Smith-Hubbard home, Bladborough Grange.

At last Hubert Palmer had to agree.

'Oh, very well,' he allowed ungraciously, as if he were threatening someone.

Hubert Palmer's bad manners were untypical. What lay behind them was anxiety and dread. He knew, and so did his wife, that the Smith-Hubbards ran a mink farm.

They were afraid that Andrew would take issue with his host and hostess at Bladborough Grange, because they bred mink to be killed, skinned and made into fur coats.

But the Palmers were at a loss as to how to extricate themselves from potential disaster. Excusatory lies were out of the question: Andrew would not let any white lie of theirs come between him and the wolfhounds. They must grin and bear the visit and hope for the best.

On the road to Bladborough Grange they dinned into Andrew yet again that the Smith-Hubbards were good kind people, whose grey hairs entitled them to the greatest respect.

There was no trouble until they were almost taking their leave two hours later on. Andrew had played with the wolfhounds and with another Smith-Hubbard dog, a Staffordshire bull-terrier called Spot, before tea. He had chased Finn and Catty for miles, sat on their rough-haired grey backs, embraced their benevolently smiling faces, and engaged in jolly mock-fights with Spot. Mrs Smith-Hubbard then spoilt him with a boiled egg at teatime, and he consumed enormous quantities of her home-baked bread and runny strawberry jam and cream-filled sponge-cake. Herbert and Grace Palmer were relieved to observe the gentlemanly behaviour of their Andrew, and gratified by the obvious fact that he was approved of by representatives of an older generation. At half-past five or so Major Smith-Hubbard, saying he had a surprise in store for Andrew, steered the party out of the stone-flagged kitchen, through the walled kitchen garden and across a small paddock to an elongated wooden shed, from which emanated an inharmonious high-pitched squeaking and squealing and a powerfully offensive acrid smell. He ushered them into it, making sure the dogs stayed outside, and shut the door.

They were in the main building of the mink farm: a few slightly sinister smaller sheds were tacked on to it at

right-angles. Light filtered dimly through dusty sky-
lights; cages, rather like big rabbit hutches, lined the four
walls at waist-height; and the mink with bright black eyes
and lustrous brown coats scrabbled at and clung to their
wire-netted windows. The noise and the stink were
awful: Mrs Smith-Hubbard covered an ear with one hand
and held her nose with the other. A workman was now
distinguishable, standing in a side-doorway: he was
middle-aged, flat-capped, dust-coloured, and the Major
bellowed that his name was Jack.

Meanwhile Andrew had approached the cages and was
reaching out his hands towards the animals: which gestures caused consternation. He was restrained by both
Smith-Hubbards and warned that the mink would bite
off any finger or fingers poked through the wire-netting;
while Jack, who wore leather gauntlets as if to prove his
employers' point, beckoned the boy. Everybody followed
Jack and Andrew into a smaller quieter shed housing
young mink.

These so-called kittens were about six to eight inches
long plus another three or four inches of tail – the adults
were between fourteen and eighteen inches plus tail.
They were attractively bold and curious, they gambolled
amongst the hay and sawdust in their cages, and displayed the usual charms of youth. At the same time they
were as sinuous as snakes, and the quickness of their movements defied and alarmed the eye. Jack said they were
savage beasts and, when Andrew asked if he could hold
one, replied with bucolic satire: 'Not half! Not likely!'

Fish was cooking in a cauldron on a primus stove for
the kittens' supper. Its smell, added to the others, was
quite asphyxiating; and the Smith-Hubbards escorted
their guests back into the paddock and the fresh air.

Andrew trotted along beside Major Smith-Hubbard, asking questions. He was told that the sheds contained about five hundred mink, that Jack fed them three times a day, and locked them in at night – or was meant to – because they were worth a heck of a lot of money. How fierce were they really? They were the bloodthirstiest little beggars, according to the Major, and absolutely fearless.

Goodbyes were exchanged on the gravel sweep in front of Bladborough Grange. Herbert and Gwen Palmer thanked the Smith-Hubbards for their hospitality and bundled Andrew into the car as hurriedly as politeness allowed.

But Andrew had one more question, crucial and over-due, to ask.

'Major Smith-Hubbard, why do you keep the mink?'

'We keep them for their pelts. Their pelts are our bread and butter. Goodbye – come again!'

Andrew forced his parents to explain everything, and was duly horrified and outraged. He said he was a fool not to have realised that the shed full of mink was just a slaughterhouse. As he saw it, beautiful wild creatures were captured, imprisoned there, permitted only to multiply, and prematurely killed in order to provide an inessential luxury garment for rich selfish people.

His mother and father argued in vain that a mink farm was no different from any other farm, or, possibly and for that matter, from gardens where vegetables were grown for eating or flowers were cut, that fur coats were considered a necessity in cold climates, and so there would always be demand in the marketplace for best mink fur; and that the mink at Bladborough Grange led secure and well-fed, if short, lives, and suffered far less from

204

being humanely put down than they would from being trapped.

Andrew not only dismissed and was indeed deaf to such reasoning, he blamed his parents for advancing it and, by implication, siding with the Smith-Hubbards. He ended the argument by glaring at them accusingly through the spectacles halfway down his nose and passing the judgment that he thought Major Smith-Hubbard was cruel. He got hold of another phrase and trotted it out with fanatical self-righteousness: 'Major Smith-Hubbard's a merchant of death.' He was unmoved by his father's charges of impertinence and incomprehension of the whole issue, and his mother's fears that he would make himself ill with fussing over a few silly mink.

Unexpectedly, when they got home and for the next three days, the word mink was not heard at Netherzoy House. Andrew at last seemed to have come to terms with the general rule of the survival of the fittest.

Then, on the next Sunday morning, his father had an accident while shaving. He sliced a piece off his chin and poured with blood. He had been listening to an early news bulletin on local radio and had heard that the mink farm at Bladborough Grange had been broken into and the animals released.

Andrew had done it.

When his father burst into his bedroom and woke him, he confessed at once and with satisfaction. The previous Saturday evening, instead of going to bed, he related, he had bicycled the four miles to and from Bladborough Grange, walked across a field or two, entered the mink

205

shed through the unlocked door and let the prisoners go.

Herbert noticed a handkerchief wound round the boy's left hand: what was the handkerchief in aid of?

One of the mink had bitten him, Andrew said.

'Serves you right,' his father commented and, having issued promises of punishment, retreated to consult his wife and get his chin seen to.

By nine o'clock Herbert and Gwen had decided to inform the Smith-Hubbards. They were agreed that honesty was the best policy – and the only one, since Andrew could not be relied upon to keep quiet about his self-styled errand of mercy.

The telephone call to Bladborough Grange was fraught with awful shocks.

Major Smith-Hubbard was out, and had been for three hours, searching for his mink: Herbert Palmer had to speak to Mrs Smith-Hubbard.

He revealed the name of the culprit and expressed heartfelt apologies, whereupon she burst into pained and prolonged tears.

Eventually she enquired feebly: 'Andrew? But we thought Andrew was our friend. Why would Andrew want to hurt us so?'

Her next equally unanswerable question was: 'Is he delinquent? If he has these criminal tendencies, perhaps you shouldn't have brought him over here. Perhaps you should have warned us.'

Then she said: 'Of course it was partly Jack's fault. He left the door unlocked. He was always forgetting to lock it. That's why he's been given the sack.'

She began to cry again, and continued: 'We're ruined, you know. We put nearly every penny we had into the farm. The insurance people won't pay up because the

206

mink were unattended and not locked in. We shan't be able to carry on in this house; and it's not as if we were young. We'll have to find the money somewhere.'

Herbert seized his first opportunity to say a sympathetic goodbye, rejoined Gwen and Andrew, who were sitting in antagonistic silence in the kitchen; and relayed the news and views of Mrs Smith-Hubbard.

Trembling and with a white face he explained that they – himself, his wife and son and heir – were obviously going to have to pay the price of every single missing mink. They were honour bound, if not bound by law, he declared, probably to hand over more cash by way of compensation than they possessed. In other words and more than likely, they would have to sell Netherzoy House to raise the money, then move into a humbler home.

The telephone rang. Herbert trotted towards the sitting-room to answer it. Gwen followed him supportively, while Andrew hung back, now looking almost as sick as his father.

It was Major Smith-Hubbard on the line, sounding tired and hoarse. He wanted to thank Herbert, and have thanks conveyed to Andrew, for – in his phraseology – coming clean about the mink.

He was generous enough to say that he did not blame the boy: 'I showed him round the farm after all. And he's an animal-lover, and I expect he thought he was being kind to our animals by coming over here and letting them out of their cages. He's too young to know the way of the world, or appreciate the damage they're bound to do to the countryside. Well, yes, he'll have to learn to respect other people's property; but I don't suppose he realised what the mink meant to us.'

Had any been recaptured, Herbert asked.

'I'm afraid not. If mink were easy to catch, their fur would never have become so expensive. I've got a nasty feeling that the dogs might have eaten a few of the kittens.'

'Do you need help, Major? Would it help if we joined in the search?'

'No, thanks. I'll be going out again shortly. But my last faint hope is that one or two of the starving mink may return to the farm for food. Otherwise it's now just a question of counting our losses.'

When Herbert haltingly offered to cover and make good those losses, Major Smith-Hubbard thanked him yet again, but added rather chillingly that the trouble and expense of litigation would thus be saved.

At least their goodbyes were friendly; and then Gwen tried to convince Herbert that his financial liability could turn out to be less damaging than he feared.

In the middle of the morning, after a couple of hours of juggling figures, they noticed Andrew's absence, discovered that his bicycle was not where it should have been, began to worry about him, and then received another call from Bladborough Grange.

Mrs Smith-Hubbard asked them to come over to fetch Andrew, who was all right but hurt, and in need of parental care and attention. Apparently he had sought out Jack, he had intended to sympathise over the disgrace and dismissal of Jack, who had given him a punitive beating for his pains.

'No doubt your son means well,' Mrs Smith-Hubbard quavered uncertainly, 'but he did deserve to have a little sense knocked into his head. I'm sure he thinks we're wicked, too, to have got rid of Jack. But how could we afford to employ Jack without any money coming in from the mink farm? And what on earth would he have to do without the mink to look after?'

The Palmers drove to Bladborough Grange. Andrew had two black eyes and was covered with blood and bruises, and his bike was all twisted out of shape. They bundled him into the car and at home put him to bed, where, with the help of painkillers, he slept until the evening.

He woke in a feverish state. His left hand, bitten by a mink twenty-four hours previously, and unnoticed in the confusion of the last twelve, had blown up like a balloon and begun to poison his whole system.

Andrew developed septicemia and was ill for months. His formal education was interrupted and, although he learned some hard lessons, his future prospects were affected adversely. But he recovered his health in the end.

Major Smith-Hubbard was not so lucky. As a result of the shock and his exertions, searching for his mink and finding none, he suffered the first of several heart attacks, which disabled and then were the death of him.

Mrs Smith-Hubbard, thanks to money received from the Palmers, was able to stay on at Bladborough Grange with the wolfhound Catty and the terrier Spot.

Herbert and Gwen and Andrew never knew if, or when, she expired there. Having sold Netherzoy House with its tree-lined drive, walled garden and paddock, they moved out of the neighbourhood and into a bungalow in the suburbs of Ilfracombe. But they did hear that Jack died prematurely of unemployment and drink, and they were again sorry.

*

Finn was amongst the first of the animal casualties of Andrew's juvenile compassion.

On the morning after the night when the mink were released, the three Smith-Hubbard dogs were let out as usual into the paddock behind the Grange. They saw and scented the mink kittens scampering about in the grass and began to chase them. Finn got excited by the sport – he seemed to be amused by the yards it took him to turn a corner which was turned by his quarry in inches. At last, almost by accident, he snapped up one of the little wriggling creatures in his huge jaws and swallowed it whole. The consequence was that lethal digestive malady to which wolfhounds are prone, called 'bloat'. He died painfully, and was mourned in varying degrees by everyone who had known him. His appearance and his character were equally noble.

Catty also chased the kittens, but in vain. On the other hand Spot, the agile bull-terrier, must have caught a dozen. He shook them to death like rats, and even munched and ate a few without ill effects on his tough constitution.

All the remaining kittens perished more or less unpleasantly. They were run over by cars on the road, they starved or were pecked to death by crows and magpies, they were devoured by foxes or stamped on by village boys.

About half the adults also met ends more disagreeable than the one reserved for them at the mink farm: to wit, sedative pills in a final feed, and death by gassing. In the unknown and unwelcoming wild, they mostly starved in a matter of a week or a fortnight.

The rest, the fitter ones, perhaps two hundred of them, survived for a little longer, and a hundred of that number

210

flourished and in due course reproduced themselves, multiplied and spread geographically.

This last group was as intelligent and resourceful as it was hardy. It was completely omnivorous and probably cannibalistic. It ate roots if meat was unobtainable, and learnt to, and dared to, steal from dustbins. It was quite prepared to fight, and often killed, cats, small dogs, otters. And although it shunned humankind, and skulked about furtively, it would attack man when cornered.

The so-called liberation of the mink from Bladborough Grange was newsworthy. The Smith-Hubbards and the Palmers spoilt some of the fun by managing to convince the press that Andrew was responsible more by accident than design. The local media, thus denied the opportunity to praise a young crusader or pillory a hooligan, made do with stories that appealed to sentimental souls and class warriors: sweet pretty furry creatures with every right to live their lives would no longer be bumped off for the greater glory of the whores of capitalism. The next journalistic trick was to introduce controversy into the issue: publish letters from town-dwelling spinsters, rejoicing over the addition of mink to the wild life of the area, alongside the apprehensive opinions of countrymen and naturalists. Then, and thereafter, the crimes of the mink could be broadcast in shocked and rabble-rousing accents.

The amphibious mink soon found the rivers and ate the fish. They could climb trees, and caught and ate birds on their nests, also birds' eggs. They poached game, they stole poultry, they ate every living thing, and seemed to be able to negotiate any obstacle. One got into somebody's larder by chewing through a zinc fly-screen; another was discovered lapping cream in the locked dairy

211

of a farm; a third decided to nest in a wendy-house and bit the child that attempted to shoo it out; a fourth devoured the prize golden carp in a lily pool. And so it went on until, having laid waste a particular area, the mink temporarily slaked their thirst for blood farther afield.

Sportsmen took up arms, literally to start with, against their rival predators. Why should mink enjoy the sport that sportsmen had paid through the nose for? Hunting and killing the unlicensed hunters and killers of pheasants and fish was some compensatory satisfaction. Game-keepers were instructed only to locate these vermin, which their employers could then have the pleasure of shooting.

Farmers who kept chickens also shot the mink if they could, and hung the corpses on poles to encourage others to come and pinch their produce.

But such methods of destruction, or attempted destruction, were both ineffective and wasteful. The mink were too difficult to find, and too wary; they refused to lie down and die unless shot at close range by the average twelve-bore; wounded ones were inclined to take refuge in barns and outhouses, and attack anybody who approached them, and of course their pelts, riddled with the holes made by shotgun pellets and often rotted by gangrenous wounds, were valueless.

Certain sharp-eyed 'professionals' were not slow to see the silver lining of these clouds. The trapping and poisoning of mink, and digging them out of holes and throttling them carefully, then removing and tanning and selling their unblemished skins, began in earnest. Poorer sportsmen, the nocturnal variety, had more money than usual to spend in pubs, while mink tippets and mink waistcoats encircled the necks and bodies of unlikely persons.

The first scare-story in a local paper, giving exaggerated accounts of children with noses, fingers and toes bitten off by mink which were three feet long and incurably savage, activated the 'amateurs' – that is to say, the hate brigade. Furious letters to the press, from worried parents and pet-owners, from gardeners who had no songbirds in their gardens, from squirrel-, frog- and snake-lovers, from campers and hikers and the lunatic fringe, called for mink to be wiped from the face of the earth.

During a kind of open season, when no fate was considered too bad for this latest public enemy, men and boys were encouraged to try to stone mink, shoot them with airguns, hook them with baited fishing-lines in and out of water, set dogs upon or otherwise destroy them.

Eventually the hue and cry subsided; many maimed creatures perished; the healthy specimens in the vicinity of Bladborough Grange were fewer in number; and the popular craze for doing them down was superseded.

The two or three dozen that remained were protected after a fashion by the managerial committee of an old-established otter hunt, which had recently changed its name to the Bladborough Otter and Mink Hounds. It now seemed to take thirty hounds and a small army of whippers-in, diggers-out, terriers and so on to catch and kill a single specimen of the ever cannier and more distrustful descendants of the mink farmed by Major and Mrs Smith-Hubbard.

But at least, as Andrew Palmer would have said when he was a boy, before he had come up against the law of unintended consequences – at least the mink he had released to live and to die these different deaths were free.

Perpetual Motion

'M Y DEAR ONE, my darling, last and dearest of all my children, your twenty-first birthday is almost upon us, you are about to come completely and unquestionably of age, therefore by way of a birthday present, or blessing, or bequest, I now intend, although I'm no longer a wealthy man, to make your fortune,' said the old duke.

The speaker was Alaric Egbert Beauregard, 25th Duke of Wessex, Earl of Ashford, Baron Seaford etc. The child or rather the adult he addressed was Lady Lucy Beauregard, the only issue borne him by his fifth and final divorced wife. The scene was the bedroom of the duke in that disintegrating pile of masonry known as Wessex Abbey, and the time six-thirty on a winter's evening. His Grace, who was ninety years old, sat in a deep armchair in front of a hot coal fire, wearing a red flannel dressing-gown, wrapped in rugs, drinking whisky and soda and smoking cigarettes.

He continued: 'I have been neither a good father nor a good duke, and my wives would say I was a bad husband. I must plead guilty to the serious charge of loving too many women too much, and money not enough. My life-work has been to re-distribute the wealth I inherited, a praiseworthy objective in socialistic circles, even if not appreciated by the members of my family. Love was an open drain in my experience: I speak financially. The costs of liberation from my five wives – with respect to your mother – escalated: duchesses in divorce courts tend to change sides and unite with the workers of the world in the inflationary spiral. Why did I marry them? At my age, believe me, one forgets. But little souvenirs of the sentimental past still arrive in the form of demands for cash from my various offspring. Gold and silver have I none, my personal pockets have already been picked, the cupboard is bare: I'm fed and kept half-alive by means of an annuity, in which I invested every last penny of my own several years ago. Begging letters from my children are returned to sender. I'd give them no more money even if I could – it would be wrong to enable them to follow my extravagant example. And now I refuse to see them, and to be accused of having traded family heirlooms for women's favours, and called spendthrift, wastrel and heartless miser. You'll have noticed that I make a grammatical distinction between you and my other issue: you are you and they are them. You are the achievement of my old age, you are the rose of my winter; and because your mother's second thoughts and mine led to divorce after a few months of marriage, I was spared sight and sound of your grubby and noisy childhood and youth, and feel the fonder of you in consequence. Moreover you are different in that you have so far asked me for nothing: perhaps your mother warned you that she had finally and completely cleaned me out. I have also supervised your education from a safe distance and basked in the reflected glory of your scholarship. Now I wish to reward you for nearly reaching the age of reason in such beautiful shape. Alas, as explained, I cannot give you the wherewithal that was taken from me by your half-brothers and half-sisters.

I am going to give you much much more. But, first, re-fill my glass, dear girl, and light my cigarette – and look less concerned, if you please! I'm not yet ready to end my days, long as they are at my time of life. I doubt if I could drink and smoke myself to death in the very near future. I have a plan, you see, and people with plans are inclined to survive to implement them. Shall I proceed?'

'Yes, Father.'

'I married so often because I'm an idealist. Yes – it comes back to me from far away – I kept on marrying the uniquely perfect woman, and expecting that we would make each other perfectly happy. That ideal was never attained, strange to relate. My true biography will be the old old story of sweet illusions deteriorating into disillusion, notwithstanding the little difference of my having been a duke and, once upon a time, a multi-millionaire. My duchesses had nothing to do except to be nasty to me; I was too rich to be happy and maybe too sensitive, certainly too sensitive for matrimony, although wife after wife called me every sort of beast in the witness box. Almost from infancy, my essential refuge from life was literature. I would agree with Logan Pearsall-Smith, who wrote: "People say that life is the thing, but I prefer reading." The joy of discovering I was able to read a book, and the book in question was funny and fun, retains its freshness in my memory: I was in my bed in the night-nursery here, and the book was Marryat's *Mr Midshipman Easy*. Again, I remember reading Edgar Wallace's *The Four Just Men* at my preparatory school much more clearly than I remember what I ate for lunch today: I climbed a tree on the playing fields and sat on a branch in order not to be disturbed by the madding crowd of my schoolfellows. I can recall the very smell of that book, and hear across the gulf of getting on for a century the excited beating of my heart. And my interest in the written word has proved more dependable and durable than love: the bookworm has buried the husband, and my wives have sunk into oblivion beneath a sea of printer's ink. Look at the amount of reading matter in this room! Look in the library downstairs! Yet something seems to me to have gone wrong in the literary area too; and in order to escape still more disillusionment I have abandoned my quest for the ideal in modern literature. My faint and final hope is that the time may be ripe for reaction, or even for corrective action. Another delicious cigarette, please, my little cat's-paw! Do you see any connection between the crushed idealist in me, and the fortune I have in store for you?'

'No, Father.'

'Patience will reveal it. Thank you, Lucy. My Lady Nicotine is my contemporary, and, although she may be a femme fatale, you must not disapprove of my caring for her still. Yes, patience, I was saying. But let me not linger in the minefield of definitions of art in general. I would merely whisper in passing, hoping nobody hears me and confronts me with exceptions to the rule, that I have always thought one test of the proper art which would hold a mirror up to nature is the difficulty of creating it. I am old-fashioned, and evidently, in the view of today's arbiters of matters artistic, I am also wrong. They would argue that modern art is easily created by children, and reserve their praise not so much for the originality of interpretations of nature as for the insolence of iconoclasm and the impudence of mere debunking. However, the tears invariably shed by idealists, in particular those which are bound to furrow the cheeks of superannuated bookworms, have not altogether blinded me to the main chance. We all know there are too many people in the world, more people working less and having more leisure and demanding more entertainment, for which they are prepared to pay more money than ever before: the question is, today as yesterday, in this room as in the traditional garrets of Grub Street, how to get one's hands on it? My answer to that question can, and with your co-operation will, enrich you. Whether or not you're prepared to follow my instructions remains to be decided, and whether or not you're capable of doing so remains to be seen. But your academic record confirms that you have the intelligence; I think you have the irreverent and malicious wit, and the courage and fortitude; and I know you are qualified by your breeding, looks and charm to cope with the requisite public relations. If my theories, incubated over many years, are viable, and I have not misjudged you, we shall have contributed a chapter, or at least an important footnote, to the history of art, culture, ethics, our family, this country, and the wider world which will pay you handsomely for entertaining it. Well – are you with me, yes or no?'

'Yes, Father.'

The Duke of Wessex sat in a chair covered with worn soft green leather. On his right-hand side stood an occasional table bearing a white cardboard box of flat Turkish cigarettes; red-topped matches in a circular glass container with a roughened exterior striking-surface; a large silver ashtray and a silver salver on which were a half-full tumbler, a decanter containing light brown liquid and a soda-siphon. On his left-hand side an angular reading lamp rose from a weighted base on the floor. Another small table within his reach had books piled high on it, some of which were open and stacked face downwards. There were books everywhere in the room, on the four-poster bed, on the bedside tables, in bookshelves, on the floor. The ducal toes in monogrammed blue velvet slippers peeped out from beneath the tartan rugs wrapped round sharp knees. A blotchy veiny hand reached for the tumbler at intervals, and skeletal fingers clipped cigarettes that were scarcely smoked. His Grace's countenance seemed to consist of a few wisps of hair, half-eye spectacles and a jutting grinning satirical chin.

In the corner of a great green leather sofa at a right angle to the fire sat Lady Lucy Beauregard with her legs curled up under her. The shape she was in was every bit as beautiful as her father had claimed. She had gently wavy lustrous black hair, a complexion clear and smooth as porcelain, adorable little aquiline features, glowing brown eyes, fine elegant bones and a slim trim figure. An aura of aristocracy, or perhaps it was the grace of privilege, clung to her: it was almost like a halo, although the implications of a halo were contradicted by her sophisticated seductive minxish smiles. Her scarlet shirt, the jewels at her throat, the single ear-ring and the glittering buckle of her belt reinforced her resemblance to a bird of paradise.

'Yes, Father,' she had said.

The 25th Duke of Wessex scratched the grey bristle on his protruding chin with a blanched fingernail, and resumed: 'You must write a book. You must write an exceptional book, exceptional in that it will be both good and a best-seller. Greatness I do not ask for – first books that are great are even more exceptional than you need to be. No! Your book will be good, since classy persons cannot deliberately write the bad books which generally sell best. It will be bought in remunerative quantities for three reasons: because of its goodness; more, because of its subject matter – by virtue of its vices, I was going to say; and thanks to our presentation of it, and strategy and tactics. And it will have to satisfy the artist in you by steering a practical middle course between ancient and modern definitions of art, by being true to nature and difficult to do, and by breaking down barriers and through conventional frontiers. But what can you write that's good – I mean, that has the ring of proven truth, that speaks from experience, yet converses with everyman in the vernacular of common-or-garden, as distinct from aristocratic, existence? Your experience is confined to whatever self-centred youth is able to accumulate. You know nothing of love, politics, religion and death, the preoccupations of adulthood. As for newness, is there anything new under the sun, you ask: didn't blind Homer say it all? I shall require a sip of strengthening refreshment before trying to answer your question.'

'Yes, Father.'

'Literature is fiction. I'm well aware that literature is said to include religious texts, poetry, drama, history, biography and so on. I repeat that literature actually boils down to what my nursemaid used to call "stories"; and I would admit that such "stories", if they are to rise above the level of imitative formulae, have to contain an element of newness, of what has not been done before, or done for a long time, of novelty if not originality,

221

and of surprise. Of course, life as lived is a story, too. But, notwithstanding the evidence of soap operas, a moment-by-moment account of the lives most of us live would be infinitely tedious, and apparently shapeless, and would lack the requisite novel element. An inclusive record of the chores of humanity would hold no one's interest: the detailed record of even an incomparable beauty or a victorious general cleaning their teeth morning and evening for eighty-odd years would not be much fun – the deliberate creation of boredom by sensation-seeking so-called artists has been tried and has failed. Literature, to come back to our muttons, is life concentrated and distilled, an aspect of life described from an individualistic point of view that, with difficulty and in effect, somehow shocks us. Do you follow me?'

'Yes, Father.'

'I would not presume to analyse great literature, since to understand is to equal. But, unarguably, classic literature very often, as a rule in fact, has shocked its contemporaries by means of challenge, protest, shooting a controversial line or hitting a sore spot. Masterpieces that may strike us as reasonable or positively mild were howled down in their day: Chekhov's plays and Turgenev's novels, *Tess of the d'Urbervilles, Madame Bovary*. Remember, Socrates was executed for making his contribution to literature; thousands of writers have been done to death by Marxism; and Solzhenitsyn is not the only artist to be exiled from his native land. Studying the history of literature, one gets the idea that originality is not very original unless it is offensive. A further deduction could well be that the success of a book is commensurate with its offensiveness, or, conversely, that a book which offends nobody is bound to be a flop. From this last proposition, my plan derives. Pardon the long-windedness, please, and tell me if you can stand no more of it.'

'Yes, Father.'

'Shall I continue?'

'Yes, Father.'

'You may be thinking that the book I want you to write, and books in general for that matter, are as old hat as I am. Entertainment for the masses is visual rather than literary nowadays. Moreover a visual impression has more instant appeal than a page of print; and no doubt more people have watched moving images in this century, and received such impressions, than all the people who have read books since the year dot. But what has moved those images? Behind every cinema and television screen lurks the bending author, as described by Shakespeare. Again, you may suppose that, considering the plethora of books not only in existence but being produced in ever greater quantities hourly, the search for a new subject, angle, invention, for the novelty or the novel capable of sharpening surfeited appetites, is hopeless. Genius has thought of everything through the thousands of years of universal culture; and the second-handers and second-raters have seized upon that thinking, and bowdlerised and cheapened it, and re-hashed and reheated and served it up with various garnishes ad nauseam. There's nothing left to write about, you reiterate: the Aunt Sallys have all been knocked flat. Certainly, virtue was a busted literary flush ages ago: virtue has become a yawn, and, into the bargain, poses major technical difficulties for the author attempting to describe it. Moreover vice, wickedness and evil are meaningless concepts in the age of psychology: which would ascribe the crimes of a Stalin or a

Hitler to their toilet training or an uncontrollable and therefore pardonable quirk of their unconscious minds. And the positive treatment of the Christian religion was completed by whoever wrote the Bible; while negative sacrilege and blasphemy, and the denigration of gods and prophets worshipped worldwide, and the mockery of faith and the faithful, that rich seam, which has produced pots of gold, is just about exhausted. Rabble-rousing political catch-phrases, "Man was born free and is everywhere in chains," for instance, and again, "Property is theft," are only dreamt up by fantasists once in a blue moon – and no wonder, since they are hardly worth the paper they are written on, they make no money, they only make revolutions and pointlessly maim and kill millions of harmless people. As for love, it's an absolute back-number, I know – so far as literature's concerned it really went out with the bustle, and now everybody's sick of sex. We've had every sort of sex stuffed down our throats, if you'll forgive my choice of words, throughout this pornographic century. And can there be any crime or form of violence unexploited gloatingly, heartlessly and incessantly by the media? What on earth will shock in these blasé days? Pain and grief are like the poor – in the artistic context they have always been with us. Homosexuality has nothing more to confess and no more ridicule to heap upon heterosexuality. Drugs and disease are stale buns. Novelty itself, paradox would say, is as old as the hills. In the future, genius will probably be able to rivet our attention again in some unexpected enlightening manner. But meanwhile, for most writers, it's back to business as usual, yesterday's business, that is, you tell me. Permit me to contradict you, my child, and make you a millionairess. I'm going to give you the map to a literary Eldorado, or, at any rate, to a gilt-edged region which no writer that I've heard of has ventured to explore. I believe you can get there, because you already have the necessary experience, you've been sitting on it for twenty-one years, so to speak, and each morning, when you start writing, you'll find you have it at your fingertips. Unless I'm very much mistaken, the sensation-seeking depraved world of ours will queue up to pay you for your dirty work. I'll tantalise you no longer; but, in order to spare your blushes, I'll put my directions in the nutshell of four discreet syllables. Here they are: scatology.'

When Lucy Beauregard looked blank, the Duke of Wessex again urged her to be patient, asked for more whisky and another cigarette, and went on: 'You have no doubt come across the German word "Bildungsroman", meaning a fictional account of growth and development. I would suggest that your book should be a "Bildungsroman", if only because the word includes the relevant letters of the alphabet – d - u - n - g. Yes! I'm telling you to write history that hits below the belt, or the story of twenty-one years of your relationship with the water closet. It will be the fullest possible study of excreta from infancy to adulthood, and from an existential rather than a scientific standpoint – life recorded and interpreted by reference to the colon, and to the smells, consistency and quantity of its waste products. You could call it a bug's eye view of humanity from the lavatory bowl, or, in even more vulgar parlance, from the bottom up. I believe I've already and privately made my point, for you look shocked. Am I right?'

'Yes, Father.'

'Overcome your native modesty, conquer your prudishness and squeamishness, break the restrictive bonds of decency, be modern! Don't be embarrassed by my stooping to such low conversation, and by as it were dipping my grey hairs in the effluent: remember today's excuse for uncouth manners and rough behaviour of every kind, "We're all in it!" Let me also jog your memory about the idealistic purpose of our undertaking, which mustn't be compromised by half-hearted and weak-kneed scruples. Unless the book is sufficiently bad it will do no good, it won't have the effect of "aversion therapy", instead of disgusting public opinion it'll seem to set another dish of piquant filth before it, and the media will have no reason to cook up more wholesome fare. Hide your eyes, if you like, but lend me your ears! And pardon my brusque imperatives – a man of my age can't afford to dawdle! Begin the book with what we do in – and out of – our nappies; proceed to the triumphs and tragedies of the potty; deal with the manic-depressive dangers of irregular digestion and evacuation; list the illnesses, neuroses, sorrows, frustration and rage caused by constipation. Laxatives and their effects will have to be closely examined. Number One as well as Number Two should be mulled over: how Number One is scented by our consumption of asparagus, for instance, and tinted by the vitamins in cooked liver, and turned into a passable imitation of brown ale by jaundice. Urinals, and the receptacles into which men and women are expected to empty their bladders in beds of sickness, could be compared with the stranger vessels and desti-

226

nations towards which urine is directed by love in its more perversely inventive moods. Yet a solid takes precedence over a liquid – which reminds me that my glass is nearly empty. Fill it, my precious angel, please!'

'Yes, Father.'

'I was going to say that you may find more to get your teeth into in solids. Unnatural love – I mean the complicated sexual rites practised by some human beings and never by animals – a popular literary subject – unnatural love has a field day with faeces. I fear you will have to soil your hands with the books written by sex therapists, and contaminate your imagination. And I suppose you'll have to chronicle once more the romantic dreams that homosexuals weave around the seat of their affections. But remember that a story is told about a hero or a heroine; whence my suggestion that your protagonist should be a sort of hermaphrodite, since sex is actually an inessential part of your narrative, and you'll profit from steering clear of inter-sexual politics. This person – or "it", for the sake of brevity – will have to be an alimentary tube, only vaguely human, every thought, emotion and sensation of which derives from the processes of ingestion and digestion. The action will be exclusively intestinal, and purple passages can describe the relief of bed-wetting; the terror and the shame of being taken short in a more serious sense in the waking state; the drama of diarrhoea; and the pride and glory of having shed a heavy load. You must imply, argue and convince us that "its" obsession is representative, that every one of us spends a large proportion of our lives either in or on the lavatory, or worrying because we're not there. The obsessiveness might be conveyed graphically by "its" attitude in church, where "it" prays not "O Lord, open thou

227

our lips," but "O Lord, open thou our bowels"; and where it is then distracted by consideration of the possible sanitary arrangements in the next world.

'The crowning glory and climax of your book, as I see it, could be an attack of gastric flu. The gathering storm in the stomach, the rumblings and gripes, the rush of wind, the stabs of pain and mounting fever would generate in almost every reader pity and terror heightened by reminiscence. The liquefaction of the entrails, the dark night of colonic agitation, the cloacal agony, horror piled upon horror in various senses, weaken the very will to live. At last the vile virus bows out. The afflicted one is again able to take nourishment without having it taken, and to sleep without having suddenly to sprint anywhere. The sting in the tail of convalescence is desperation owing to the alternative experience of a suspected internal blockage: nothing gets done for days on end. But relief finally arrives: a bit like an annunciation, announcing better things to come. Clouds assume a lining not exactly silver, encouraging nonetheless, and the ending is happy inasmuch as regularity is regained and "it" decides life is worth living after all.'

The Duke of Wessex coughed feebly after talking so much, and seemed on the point of expiry. But he restrained Lucy from summoning assistance, pointed to his glass of whisky, and, when she had helped him to sip from it, he caught his breath and eventually spoke again.

'The title of your book is inevitable and obvious: it has to be called *Perpetual Motion*. However, in the mean-

228

while, I note the sceptical expression on your pale face. Are you afraid that not many people will pay to read the stuff I want you to write?'

'Yes, Father.'

'Reading has little or nothing to do with the success of books. How many people ever read Rousseau's *Du Contrast Social* or Marx's *Das Kapital*, which revolutionised – and terminated – billions of lives, or, for that matter, the best-seller of all time, namely Holy Writ? How many have read right through the great books of the twentieth century, *A La Recherche du Temps Perdu* and *The Gulag Archipelago*? One wonders if adults really read anything. Exhaustive research has convinced me that the most successful books are those which are not read much, and that they are always outrageous, they always outrage someone, or some religion or nation or class or tradition or convention. Furthermore, the success of a book is surely created not by its writer, but by intermediaries, disciples, commentators, and its victims. The errors of the King and Queen of France made Rousseau's shallow epigrams look like a viable political programme, and the reserved and rigid helplessness of the Tsar and Tsarina of Russia made Marx's academic bombast look like the solution of the problems of their subjects. The success of *Gone with the Wind* was multiplied many times by the film of the book. But of course you're right. Your study of excrement and excretion would not succeed in all probability if published as if it were any old book, notwithstanding the attractions of the subject and the predictable excellence of its presentation. However, may I now explain, without casting the slightest aspersion on your abilities, that the book under discussion was never meant to be more than the first part of my plan?'

'Yes, Father.'

'The dual object of the exercise is to make money and, secondly, poke fun at fashionable writing, publishing and readers. Your wealth will be earned by a combination of your talents and my knowledge of the foibles of my fellows in general and my countrymen in particular. Let's suppose *Perpetual Motion* has been written: I've already chosen its publisher. Vulture Books is sufficiently large, international, amoral and venal for our purposes. The typescript of your book must bear no author's name: we'll get it sent to Vulture Books and in due course strike a record bargain without the help of lazy and greedy middlemen. But, you say, hard-boiled publishers won't be impressed by the hoary old confidence trick of anonymous authorship. Not so, I reply: any British publisher, any true blue British snob in publishing, will sit up very straight when he or she sees that the typescript was despatched from the Estate Office of the Dukedom of Wessex. But, you say again with commendable cynicism or realism, the average publisher won't be keen to publish a book, however ducal, that differs from other books. I must agree; therefore my Estate Office will have posted two further copies of the typescript, one to the most puritanical of the prelates who love publicity, and the other to the most liberal and permissive of politicians. The churchman's bound to inveigh against the indecency of the book, and sermonise about it being a symptom of the decline of moral standards, of decadence and loss of faith in religion. The politician's equally certain to take issue with these opinions, and avail himself of the opportunity to fulminate against clerical and general conservatism, and call anyone wishing to censor the book a foul fascist. Both will throw the petrol of class onto the fire

230

of their argument: they will blame the arrogance of a duke too cowardly to speak his name, the irresponsibility of the upper crust, the frivolity of the idle rich, for attempting to corrupt the honest proletariat. Then the media are going to compete to buy a slice of profitable trouble. The vultures of Vulture Books and the communications industry, scenting blood or blood-money, are going to fight over the corpse of the carrion of your literary labours. The nastier the public stink the more money you'll be paid for causing it – advances of royalties, serialisation, paperback, translation and broadcasting rights, probably even cash for an option to base an avant-garde film on the book. And the figures of whatever you're paid will spin off another form of advertisement: "One million pounds already banked by the mysterious genius behind the ultimately controversial novel," or else, "One million reasons why *Perpetual Motion* must be the best book ever written." Your success is assured in accordance with the law of the modern literary jungle: no book succeeds like that which has earned big pre-publication money, since it has to be sold somehow, by hook or by crook, by bribery and corruption, by "plugging" and "hype", in order to make sure its backers recover their investment. "Spot the missing author" could be the basis of the next advertising campaign – "Who is he, who is she?" – reinforced by a reward offered for the discovery of your identity and a bonus for finding you. But that brings me to the part of my plan of campaign which ensures victory. Can your twenty-one years spare my ninety a few more minutes?'

'Yes, Father.'

'The fallacy of modern political thinking is the notion that revolution, any sort of revolution, evolutionary revolution, rises from the bottom of the social pile to the top. Karl Marx must have been standing on his head when he claimed that history was on the side of revolting workers. The reverse happens to be the truth. The power – the permission – behind every new political development for thousands of years, behind new cultural developments too, has been provided by the class born to rule. The French mob stormed the Bastille only because certain aristocrats suffering from social guilt patronised the agents and agencies of radicalism and played with the fire of radical ideas. The origins of the Russian revolution were the charitable intentions of representatives of the Russian aristocracy, who went slumming amongst the peasantry and thus paved a road to hell for all Russian people. In art, it's always been a case of whoever pays the piper calling the tune. The art of poor artists makes its mark insofar as it pleases the rich: witness, to cite but three examples, the arts of ancient Egypt and ancient Greece, and of the Italian Renaissance. In this context our democracy is no more democratic than the old Athenian model, which was dependent on slavery. Admittedly people seldom understand the spirit of their own age; yet I remain convinced that hierarchical forces continue to leaven the lump of today's egalitarian society. Consequently, in my estimation, when it emerges as emerge it must, since no secrets can be kept from journalists, that *Perpetual Motion* is the product of my offspring if not of myself, that it really is the destructive creation of the fruit of ducal loins, and that it was written by a slip of a girl, your charming self, the seal will be set on its success. Not only will it and you be attacked more or less violently by every inverted snob, leveller, prig and prude, and defended by their opposite numbers; not only will

232

reviewers rush to get in on the act, some doing their customary damning, while others praise the universality of the subject of the book, and the liberating frankness and the courageous condescension of its author; and not only will you achieve the sales figures of the average scandalous publication. Commercially speaking, that is to say vulgarly, the cherry on the cake will be your personal appearances in response to public demand. Please, pretty Lucy, moisten my lips once more, and light me a sundowner of a cigarette.'

'Yes, Father.'

'I repeat, and I regret, that you are going to have to submit to trial by television and the injustice of the masses. But your breeding alone will bring you the rewards of controversy: you'll be paid to be loved and hated for the accident of your birth. You will solve a little mystery by ceasing to be anonymous and by showing your face for a fee. Your girlishness and smuttiness will yield a contentious dividend. And your youth and beauty will be a titillating contrast to the contents of *Perpetual Motion*, and woo innumerable members of your audience into bookshops. May I just remind you that the ultimate test of sexual attraction is to be equally attractive to both sexes? Cut your hair a trifle shorter, wear tomboy clothes and the discreetest make-up, in order to obtain the favour of a pressure group now powerful enough to make or break any artist or artistic effort: I refer to homosexuals, female as well as male, and bisexuals. Last but by no means least, pray that heterosexual feminists, if any, show solidarity with your womanhood, and for once, for a change, do not envy and betray their successful sister and their principles.'

'There, I've done! You will or you would win by fol-

233

lowing my advice, also lose. The costs to be counted are censure, obloquy. On the other hand, remember, as I do, thinking of your remoter future, that wonders last nine days. And you will soon marry and change your name, and could sink into obscurity and oblivion if you wished to. Besides, you would enjoy that most valuable privilege of choice which only money confers; and you would have taught literature a salutary lesson by laughing at it. Good night, darling girl, learn from your poor father's errors and profit from his wealth – at any rate – of experience! I'm sorry not to be able to give you a conventional twenty-first birthday present; but I believe I can confidently wish you – and the art of letters to boot – many happy returns from doing as I say.'

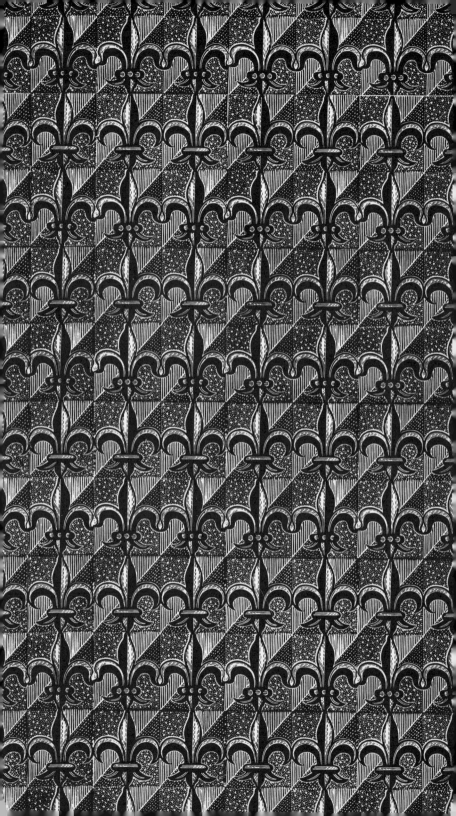